ONCE UPON A
UNICORN

ONCE UPON A
UNICORN

LOU ANDERS

CROWN BOOKS FOR YOUNG READERS
NEW YORK

Text copyright © 2020 by Louis H. Anders III
Jacket and interior art copyright © 2020 by Brian Miller

All rights reserved. Published in the United States by Crown Books for Young Readers,
an imprint of Random House Children's Books, a division of
Penguin Random House LLC, New York.

Crown and the colophon are registered trademarks of Penguin Random House LLC.

Visit us on the Web! rhcbooks.com

Educators and librarians, for a variety of teaching tools, visit us at
RHTeachersLibrarians.com

Library of Congress Cataloging-in-Publication Data
Names: Anders, Lou, author.
Title: Once upon a unicorn / Lou Anders.
Description: First edition. | New York: Crown Books for Young Readers,
an imprint of Random House Children's Books, a division of
Penguin Random House LLC [2020] |
Audience: Ages 8–12. | Audience: Grades 4–6. |
Summary: A curious, science-minded unicorn and a fiery horse
become unlikely allies as they defend their magical home
from a pumpkin-headed menace and a fairy of dubious integrity.
Identifiers: LCCN 2019057153 (print) | LCCN 2019057154 (ebook) |
ISBN 978-1-5247-1944-9 (hardcover) | ISBN 978-1-5247-1945-6 (library binding) |
ISBN 978-1-5247-1946-3 (ebook)
Subjects: CYAC: Good and evil—Fiction. | Magic—Fiction. | Friendship—Fiction. |
Unicorns—Fiction. | Fairies—Fiction. | Fantasy.
Classification: LCC PZ7.A518855 On 2020 (print) | LCC PZ7.A518855 (ebook) |
DDC [Fic]—dc23

The text of this book is set in 11.5-point Carniola.
Interior design by Cathy Bobak

Printed in the United States of America
10 9 8 7 6 5 4 3 2 1
First Edition

FOR ALEX

CONTENTS

ONCE UPON A
UNICORN

PROLOGUE

THAT'S A UNICORN FOR YOU

This is a story about a unicorn.

You know what a unicorn is, right?

Horse with a horn on its head. Everyone thinks they're pretty. And oh so *good.*

Unicorns are, like, the goodest of good creatures.

Just a big gallon of goodness in the shape of a horse.

With a horn on its head.

A *magic* horn.

A horn that can heal just about anything.

That's a unicorn for you.

And this is a story about a unicorn.

But this is also a story about a night mare.

Not a nightmare, silly. Pay attention, you!

No, a night *mare*.

Mare as in the word for a girl horse. A night mare.

You know what that is, right?

No?

You've seen them, though, I imagine.

Those burning horses that breathe red fire. They race through the darkness with their hooves aflame! They strike wicked sparks from the ground at every step. Step! Step! Step! Spark! Spark! Spark!

They're snorty, and scary, and wild. And they give you the heebie-jeebies.

Because it's the night mares that cause your nightmares. It happens like this: One runs past you when you're sleeping. It poisons your dreams, and then you're crying for mommy.

That's a night mare.

There's one of those in our story too.

Pretty scary, huh?

So this is a story about a unicorn *and* a night mare.

Together.

Because of course they're going to meet. And that's

going to be a problem for both of them. Unicorns and night mares don't get along. Not at all. In fact, unicorns and night mares fight whenever they see each other.

Which they do fairly often, because they're in the same place. Or near enough.

Right now, they all live in a magical realm called the Glistening Isles.

Glistening.

It means the shine of something wet and sparkly.

Where are these isles?

Somewhere west of here. Probably. Or maybe it's east of there. It doesn't matter. You can't get there from here.

Only I know how to get there. And I'm not going to tell you. But I will tell you *about* it. If you listen.

See, it all started like this.

A long time ago, the unicorns wandered the world. These beautiful, wild creatures lived in the beautiful, wild places. Sometimes you'd see them on the hillside at night. Maybe you were traveling on a lonely road. You'd feel something odd in the air—something tingling, something magical. Then you'd look and there they were. Under the moons. Looking all silvery and gorgeous and good. Like a vision. A spirit. A creature made of magic and myth.

Sometimes the unicorns would appear to young girls, and sometimes they would appear to brave knights, and sometimes, just sometimes, they would appear in a time of need.

So if you were hurt, a unicorn might appear and heal you. Maybe you slipped and fell in the woods and cut your leg on a sharp stone. Or maybe you were gored by a stag or a rhinoceros or a wombat or something. I don't know what you get up to. But there you are, all bleedy and weepy, and suddenly you smell that magic. You feel that tingle. And then a unicorn would appear out of nowhere. They'd come trotting up, and their horn would get all golden glowy and when it touched you—presto!—you'd be all better. No more hurt. No more blood. No more ick. Maybe not even a scar.

That's a unicorn for you. A unicorn could heal just about anything.

Some folks even said a unicorn horn could heal a broken heart. Now, I don't know if that's true, but one thing is certain. Unicorn horns are powerful stuff. *POWERFUL.*

But then some greedy people thought, why wait for the unicorns to come trotting up smelling of magic? What if they don't come? What if they go somewhere else and take their horns with them? What if someone else gets them first? What then, huh?

So they did what people love to do with things that are special and valuable and precious and rare.

They hunted them.

They hunted unicorns to chop off their horns to make magic wands to wave about. They hunted unicorns to lop off their horns and grind them into powder to sprinkle in their oatmeal and salt in their soup to cure their warts and ease their tummies and make the hair grow on their chins or stop it growing on their backs. They wanted the horns to ease their blisters and shrink their corns, to make their noses dry and their farts smell better. Or whatever silly thing they thought it would do.

What of the poor unicorns? They were chased all over the lands until there were fewer and fewer and fewer. And fewer still.

Somebody said that if it didn't stop soon, why, one day there'd be no unicorns at all. Everybody knew that and said what a shame it would be, but nobody stopped. They just kept right on hunting.

And the number of unicorns in the world got smaller and smaller and smaller.

But then something happened.

They disappeared. Every last one of them.

People looked everywhere, but they were gone. Gone, gone, gone.

No one knew where they went.

Well, almost no one.

You see, a fairy queen—a very powerful, beautiful,

and probably *mostly* good fairy queen—felt sorry for the unicorns. She said, "Come and live with me, where you'll always be pretty and happy and safe. You can prance and dance about on my perfectly manicured green lawns, and I can look at you all I want, and you can be beautiful all you want. And no one will hunt you for your horn. And I'll only ride you on special fairy holidays. And there'll be flowers and marshmallows. Doesn't that sound wonderful?"

Well, the unicorns must have thought so, or mostly so, because they all agreed.

So that very day, she brought them to her realm. A hidden place called the Glistening Isles. It was there on the biggest island where she ruled over her court, which was called the Court of Flowers. There was sun and green meadows. And as you might imagine, there were lots and lots of flowers—several of which were very tasty. After she took the unicorns, the queen put a fog around the islands to hide them. Then she charmed the Sea Saw Serpent, that great big beastly bane of boats, telling it to swim circles round and round the islands forever, and to saw any boats that sailed into her waters in two and to eat any sailors who came looking for *her unicorns.*

Because they were *her* unicorns now. Make no mistake. They were all hers and no one else's.

But that's okay, because she's a *good* fairy queen.

Mostly good. Good enough, I suppose.

But on the other side of the big island, the south side, well, if you ever find yourself on the Glistening Isles, which you never will, because you don't know how to get there, but if you ever do, don't go to the south side.

That's the Whisperwood, home to the Court of Thistles, where the Wicked Fairies are.

It's a place of darkness and thorns, and weeds, and bent twisted trees, and grasping vines, and foul-tasting mushrooms, and cold shadows where the sun never really shines. And Wicked Fairy Creatures. And ghosts, probably. And ghouls, most certainly. And long-legged beasties, it's a good bet.

Oh, and then there's Jack o' the Hunt.

Jack o' the Hunt. O'. As in "of."

Jack o' the Hunt.

Who's he?

We'll get to him later. Just remember the name Jack o' the Hunt.

But the Whisperwood was home to other creatures too. By which I mean the night mares.

Sometime after the queen brought the unicorns to the Glistening Isles, the night mares appeared as well.

It was a mystery how they got there. Did someone bring them? No one really knows where night mares come from.

But appear they did. *Pop. Pop. Pop.* With their snorty nostrils and their flaming feet. Breathing smoke and stirring up bad dreams among the unicorns and the mostly good fairies. And generally being unpleasant.

And the unicorns didn't like it. Not one bit.

So they made certain that the night mares stayed in the Whisperwood and never left it. Far from the green grass and rolling hills and sunny skies of the Court of Flowers: the best for the unicorns, the rest for them.

Did the night mares like the Whisperwood, with its twisted trees and monstrous Wicked Fairies? And mushrooms and shadows? Nobody ever asked them.

What do you think? Would you enjoy being stuck in the Whisperwood? Never to see the sun or smell the flowers? Eating only thorns and thistles and mushrooms and moss?

Of course you wouldn't.

You'd say, "Things are going to have to change around here, aren't they?"

Of course they are. But saying you need a change and actually making a change are two different things. And the one is a lot easier than the other.

So how will things change? How?

And who will change them?

Curious? Well, read the next page.

1

FOOLISH FIRE FUMBLING

Something dark moved through the Whisperwood. It was Midnight.

No, I don't mean it was midnight on the clock. It was actually a few hours before then. And, anyway, clocks weren't really a thing in these parts.

No, I mean the something dark moving through the woods *was* Midnight.

Midnight, a young night mare. A yearling nearly two years old. (That's nearly twelve for a human, just so you know.)

Watch how she walks. See how fearless and bold she moves? There's no fear in her. Not a drip. Not a drop. Not a snizzle.

Hmmm . . .

Do you think that she's maybe being a little foolish as she struts so confidently through the twisted trees and deep shadows?

Well, she is.

And you'd be right if you guessed that she was very brash and stubborn and oh so very assertive for her age.

Too big for her bridle, you might say, if anyone ever bridled a night mare. But they didn't. The bridle would just burn up.

In Midnight's case, however, it would probably sizzle, spark, and *explode*.

Because Midnight's fire was Wild.

Her fire shot out in all directions when she was excited. Or angry. Or giddy. Or hiccupy. Or just bored.

Like the time she belched and a burst of flame set Old Sooty's tail on fire. It had been very funny for everyone. Well, not for Old Sooty. Actually, it had only been funny for Midnight. The rest of the herd weren't exactly what you'd call *amused*.

Then there was the time she stamped her feet and fried a whole patch of mushrooms to a crisp. No one, not even Midnight, had thought that was very funny. The herd had gone hungry then, because mushrooms are what you eat in the Whisperwood, where no grass grows and no wheat sprouts. Naturally, burning up everyone's dinner didn't earn her any love.

In fact, Midnight's uncontrollable fire was a bit of a problem for the herd, really. They weren't sure what to do about her. They didn't have any ideas at all. But that was okay, because Midnight had a Plan. A Plan to fix everything.

"That's right," said Midnight. "I have a Plan."

She was cantering through the Whisperwood as if it wasn't full of dangerous, ugly, evil Fairy Creatures. She was cantering with purpose and determination.

"I wish you'd tell me what the Plan was," said her friend Vision. Vision was also a night mare, a little older than Midnight. But Vision wasn't walking with purpose. Vision wasn't so much cantering as she was slinking and slunking, as if the woods were full of dangerous, ugly, evil Fairy Creatures. Which they were.

"I can't tell you the Plan," said Midnight. "Not yet."

"Why?" asked Vision.

"Because if I told you," said Midnight, "you'd try to talk me out of it."

"That means I wouldn't like it," said Vision. "Why won't I like it? What am I doing out here, Midnight, if I won't like it?"

"You're out here," said Midnight, "because you're the only one crazy enough to go with me when I am being me."

"Oh," said Vision. She was about to say more, but it was true. When Midnight was being Midnight nobody was crazy enough to come along, except maybe Vision. Everyone else would just roll their eyes and maybe stand a little bit away in case anything exploded.

Vision was wondering why she had to always be the one to go with Midnight, when both horses heard something go *scuttle, scuttle, scuttle* in the darkness to their left.

"We should go back," said Vision. "We should never have left the Silent Stones at night."

"We will go back," said Midnight. "Just after we've put my Plan into effect. And, anyway, the Silent Stones are why we're out here."

Now, Dear Reader, I'm betting you don't know what the Silent Stones are. That's okay. Don't feel bad. No human has ever seen them. At least, not for a long, long time. Not since they were called the Singing Stones, and you weren't around back then. You'll learn more about them later. For now, just know that they are a big circle of stones, and that Wicked Fairies and Wicked Fairy Creatures don't like coming close to them. So at night, when the Wicked Fairies and the Wicked Fairy Creatures are at their worst, the herd of night mares sleeps in the circle of the Silent Stones.

And they never, never leave them until the dim light that passes for morning in the Whisperwood comes worming its way through the twisted branches overhead.

Which is why Vision was frightened and Midnight was very, very foolish.

But if she wasn't being foolish, well, then nothing was ever going to change.

And things needed to change. So keep reading.

And stop interrupting.

Because in all the time we've been talking Midnight and Vision have wandered very far from the stones indeed. And something has wandered after them.

Scuttle, scuttle, scuttle, went the noise again. This time to their left.

"What's that?" said Vision.

"It's a noise," said Midnight. And she wasn't wrong. But she wasn't exactly right.

"Yes, I know it's a noise," snapped Vision. "I mean what made the noise?"

"Something," said Midnight. "Something made the noise. But we're after something else."

"But it could be dangerous," said Vision. "Aren't you even curious what it is?"

"I am not curious," said Midnight. "I do not have time to be curious. I am on a mission because I have a Plan."

"Which you won't tell me. Because I'll talk you out of it."

"Because it will spoil the—"

"Surprise!" cried a voice from the trees.

Suddenly, a thick and sticky spiderweb, like the biggest spiderweb you never saw, fell from above and landed on Vision.

Vision cried out, but she was trapped like a fat fly. Like a horse fly, I suppose you could say.

You could say that, but please don't. That's a very bad pun. And it's in poor taste to pun when someone is in danger.

Meanwhile, Vision was thrashing and bashing, but she was stuck fast.

Midnight looked up in the branches, and there she saw a nasty fairy. It was a *sprider.* A sort of sprite spider. About the size of a small dog. But nothing like a dog at all, unless of course the dog had eight hairy limbs, wicked teeth, too many eyes, and could shoot webbing from its bottom. Who'd want a dog like that?

"Help, help!" cried Vision.

Midnight snorted. Both because Vision wasn't being brave and because a single sprider was just a nuisance. Not a serious danger.

And also because Midnight was summoning her fire.

A big gout of red flame belched from Midnight's mouth. The fire struck the sprider web and burned it up. The flame raced up the webbing and burned the fairy monster on its bottom.

It yelped and leapt higher into the branches.

Scuttle . . . scuttle . . . scuttle . . . They could hear it racing away.

"See," said Midnight. "Nothing to worry about."

"Nothing to worry about?" said Vision. "I was very nearly dinner."

"You weren't," said Midnight. "And anyway, I think spriders are nocturnal. So you would have been more like breakfast."

"That doesn't make it better," said Vision. "I don't want to be anyone's breakfast or dinner. I don't want to be out here after dark at all."

"I'm sorry," said Midnight. "But this really is important."

"I know, the Plan."

"You don't know the Plan," said Midnight. "Only I know the Plan."

"No, what I mean is—"

"There it is!" yelled Midnight in excitement. "Look."

Vision looked and saw a weird, wispy, glowing blue light shining some distance away through the woods. It was almost too far to see. Almost. But not quite. Midnight couldn't be after one of those, could she?

She could!

"Don't let it get away!" yelled Midnight.

"Wait," Vision said. But Midnight didn't wait. She took off.

Vision watched her go for a moment. Then she ran after her friend. Chasing after Midnight was better than being alone in the Whisperwood at night.

But she wasn't alone.

There was a pumpkin patch just a few paces from them. And in the patch was a pumpkin, just as you might expect. But there was one thing about it you wouldn't expect.

The pumpkin was watching the night mares.

Watching? How could a pumpkin do that?

How could a pumpkin do anything?

This one could. This one did.

Now, are you curious yet?

2

CURIOSITY KILLED THE WHAT, THEN?

Being curious can make life difficult.

Or rather, being Curious can make life difficult.

Certainly, being *with* Curious could be difficult.

What do I mean?

You've guessed it, right? The Curious I'm talking about is a *somebody*.

And not just *anybody*.

Curious was a unicorn.

Curious was a yearling. Just like Midnight. And Curious was always curious. Always. And by always I mean *always*.

As far as I know, he's the only unicorn in the herd who ever was.

Oh, unicorns could be a lot of things. Unicorns could be noble. Dignified. Glorious. They could be majestic. And all of them from the littlest filly or colt to the biggest mare or stallion thought *very highly* of themselves. Oh, yes, they did.

But one thing they weren't, they weren't curious. Why would they be?

When you know you're the best, you don't worry overmuch about the rest.

So they were *never* curious.

But Curious made up for it by being curious enough for all of them. By being the most curious unicorn ever.

And did they appreciate it?

Oh, no.

Quite the opposite. They didn't care for his curiosity one bit. In fact, they'd really prefer it if he wasn't curious at all. Because curiosity was always getting Curious into mischief. And upsetting the herd.

Like the time when Curious tried to trap a gigglepuss to see how its laugh-inducing purr actually worked. But then he accidentally-on-purpose sort of set it loose during the fairy queen's summer festival. The fuzzy, furry, funny thing ran purring right down the middle of the big parade, its tickly whiskers swiping all the unicorns' legs.

And all the stone-faced unicorns had started snickering. Then giggling. Then laughing uncontrollably. Then they were falling out of line and rolling on the ground, hooting with their hooves in the air. You should have seen it! It was ignoble. Undignified. Inglorious. It was very definitely not majestic. And it made the fairies think *very poorly* of the unicorns.

The herd had never been so embarrassed. The whole parade was ruined. Oh, the queen had been upset! She'd made it rain on them for a week! A whole week of being wet and miserable without any sunshine. And it was all Curious's fault.

Then there was the time Curious wondered about fairy doors and what was on the other side. You know about fairy doors, right? Tiny little doorways. They pop up in the trunks of very old trees or under certain rocks. You see them in the stems of mushrooms. Or shimmering in the broken gate of an old wooden fence. If you've ever glanced through one, then you know what they are. They're passageways, secret corridors from our world to Elsewhither, the land all fairies come from originally.

Well, Curious wanted to see that land. He wanted a view of Elsewhither with its so-green hills and its so-blue skies. He wanted to know how much greener and bluer things could be there than here. So he crouched down as low as he could and peered into a door that had materialized in a tree stump for a good glimpse of Elsewhither. Only he couldn't see very well, so he decided to stick his head in. But what you stick might get stuck. And wouldn't you know it, he got his head stuck. For a whole day. And part of a night.

You'd think he wouldn't be curious anymore after that, but you'd be wrong. He was as curious as ever.

"Oh, Curious," the rest of the unicorns said, "why do you have to be so curious?"

But Curious couldn't be any other way.

His friend Grace, however, could do without being curious.

Grace was just about Curious's age. She had a star-shaped marking on her forehead, right where her very large horn grew. But other than that, she was very typical for a unicorn. She was every bit as pretty and vapid as the rest of them. In fact, the only thing atypical about her was that she was out in the dark with Curious at night, instead of being curled up asleep inside the fairy ring in the glen in the middle of the Willowood with the rest of the herd. And she didn't know what she was doing there.

"It's okay," Curious assured her. "I know what I am doing."

"You always say that," said Grace.

"You do," said Wartle. "You always do."

"That's because I always know," said Curious.

"He does," said Wartle. "He always does."

"But why did you drag me out here with you?" said Grace.

"I know why he dragged me," said Wartle. "I know, I know."

Wait a minute, you're thinking. *Wartle? What's a Wartle?*

Well, it's not a wart-turtle, that's for sure.

And, obviously, it's not a unicorn. Not with a name like that. Unicorns have names like Sparkle, and Shimmer, and Radiance, and Glory, and Summersunshine, and Starlight Gl—Well, anyway, they don't have names like Wartle.

Wartle is definitely *not* a name for a unicorn.

It's definitely a name for a puckle.

Which is good, because Wartle was a puckle.

And puckles, my friend, are a nuisance. A bothersome nuisance. A blithering nuisance.

Those hairy little fairies get their noses into everything. And if they think it's shiny, they'll take it. If they think it's tasty, they'll eat it. If they think it's funny, they'll laugh at it. They're furry and smelly. They pick their nostrils and don't wash their hands after. They leave grubby little paw prints on your best tea sets, on the polished banisters of your palace, and on the gleaming glass of all your magic mirrors.

Puckles weren't evil. They weren't Wicked Fairies, but it was also hard to call them Good Fairies. The queen called them *pests. Bothersome ill-mannered little pests,* said the queen. Grace agreed with her. So did most unicorns.

21

But Curious liked them. Or at least, Curious liked Wartle.

They had met that very day when he'd gotten his head stuck in the fairy door.

Wartle had planned to come through that door to visit the Glistening Isles, and he had to wait a day and part of a night to do so. But he'd kept Curious company while Grace had run off for help. Curious had wanted to know about how there were little doors for little fairies and big doors for big fairies, and how most of the big doors were shut and most of the little doors were open. He was fascinated. And he asked all kinds of questions. Wartle had never had anyone ask him anything. In fact, he'd never before met anyone who wanted to listen to him at all. So they had talked and talked. And they had been friends ever since.

Now you might wonder, what does a unicorn get out of being friends with a puckle, and what does a puckle get from being friends with a unicorn?

For Wartle, Curious would sneak him out occasional marshmallows from the queen's palace. The queen's occasional marshmallows were the best marshmallows in the world.

And for Curious, one thing about Wartle that wasn't a nuisance was that the little hairy guy had . . .

"Hands," said Wartle. "I'm here because Curious needs my hands."

He held up his little pink paws and wiggled his fingers.

Grace blew a skeptical blast of air from her nostrils.

"You could never run a mile on those," she said. "Anyway, I really don't know why anyone would want hands when they could have hooves."

"Yeah?" said Wartle. "Try picking up one of these, then."

And with that, he reached in his little red jerkin, the one with the shiny black buttons that he always wore, and he pulled out a sparkling purple roundish gem.

Grace was so startled she whinnied.

"Curious!" she shouted. "Is that one of the queen's Absorbing Orbs?"

"Umm," replied Curious. "Will you be upset if I tell you that it is?"

"Upset?" yelled Grace. "Absolutely I'll be upset."

"I'll be sure not to tell you that, then," said Curious.

Grace whinnied again in frustration.

"You know the Orbs are off-limits! We're not supposed to touch them."

"He's not touching them," said Wartle. "I am. Hands, see?"

But Grace wasn't listening to the puckle.

"Oh, Curious," she said, "why do you have to be so curious?"

(I don't know the answer to that question either.)

"Look, I only borrowed it," Curious explained. "I need it for my Grand Experiment."

"What do you need to do grand experiments for?" said Grace. "Why do you have to go question everything? Isn't it enough that the sun is always shining and the grass is always green? Why do you have to go asking *why*?"

"Because I *want* to understand," said Curious.

"What's to understand?" said Grace. "It's the queen's magic, is all."

"Yes, but how does it work?"

"That's simple," said Grace. "Magic works by magic."

"By magic," repeated Wartle, bobbing his head.

"Yes, but how does it *work*?"

"I just told you. Magic works by magic! So now you know. Can we *please* go home?"

"No," said Curious. "Not until I've got what I need for my Experiment."

"And what is that?"

"Something rare," said Curious. "Something . . . there!" He indicated with his muzzle.

Grace looked and saw a weird, wispy glowing blue light shining some distance away through the woods. It seemed to be hovering in the air. It was almost too far to see. Almost.

"Wait," she said. "That's a wispy wood wink, isn't it?"

"Yes," said Curious.

"What's it doing outside the Whisperwood?"

"I don't know," said Curious.

"They never come this far into the queen's territory."

"I know," said Curious. "But Harmonyhoof said she saw one last night, and there it is."

"Oh, I get it! I get it!" said Wartle. "That's what the Absorbing Orb is for. The fairy queen uses it to store light for the night, and you're going to use it to trap a wispy wood wink so you can study it!"

"Exactly," said Curious. He gave Wartle the sort of approving nod a teacher might give a bright student.

"Why would you want to study it?" asked Grace.

"I want to know why it's blue."

"Because it's magic," said Grace. "That's why."

Curious sighed and explained. "Not all magic is blue," he said. "The queen's magic is more purply. The Wicked Fairy magic is black. When our horns heal a hurt, they glow golden. And a night mare's fires burn orange and red."

"Magic comes in a rainbow of colors. So what?" said Grace.

"So I want to know why," said Curious.

"But, Curious," protested Grace. "Wispy wood winks are dangerous. They lead you astray."

"I've never been to Astray," said Wartle. "Is it nice?"

"They get you lost in the woods," continued Grace. "And then they drown you in the bogs."

"Bogs?" said Wartle.

"That's only because they charm you," said Curious. "But I am immune to being charmed."

"Why are you immune?" asked Grace.

"I am immune because I have a Scientific Mind. And scientists all know how to keep themselves detached. I don't want to look at their pretty color. I want to study them objectively. Therefore, I cannot be charmed."

"I don't know," said Grace. "That doesn't sound very accurate."

"You don't understand because you are not a scientist," said Curious. "But don't fear. I am. And I know what I am doing."

"You always say that," said Grace.

"You do," said Wartle. "You always do."

Fortunately, before Curious, Grace, and Wartle could be trapped in a circular conversation, the wispy wood wink bobbed in the air and retreated.

"Quickly," said Curious. "After it."

Wartle leapt onto his back, and Curious took off at a gallop, chasing the wood wink.

"Wait! Wait!" shouted Grace as she ran after him.

"Science doesn't wait!" Curious replied.

Grace did not have a Scientific Mind, so she couldn't argue the point, but she did have an unerring sense of when Curious was heading for trouble. She galloped after him.

When she caught up with him, he had stopped. That was because the wispy wood wink had stopped too.

Grace felt the pull from its strange mesmerizing light. She turned her eyes away.

"Don't look at it," she advised him.

"It's okay, Grace," said Curious. "I have my detachment, and I won't be affected, not at all, not a bit . . . even if the wispy wood wink is . . . fascinating . . . mesmerizing . . . and . . . pretty."

"Shut your eyes, Curious," said Grace.

"Pretty," repeated Curious. His mouth hung slack and his eyelids drooped.

"Pretty, pretty, pretty," he repeated. And his Scientific Mind must not have been as good as he thought it was, because now he most definitely sounded charmed.

"Pretty, pretty," repeated Wartle where he rode atop Curious's back.

"Please, Curious," said Grace, "turn away."

But it was too late. Curious did not turn away. In fact, Curious followed the wispy wood wink as it drifted on through the night. Grace tried to stop him, but he pushed her aside. And he followed the wispy wood wink when it bobbed out over the River Restless, that churning, rushing rapid water that separated the fairy queen's land from that of the Wicked Fairies. But wispy wood winks can fly, and unicorns cannot. Not even a little.

Splash, went Curious as he fell into the swift current.

The cold water awakened his Scientific Mind, but by then it was too late.

"Help!" cried Curious.

"Help! Help!" cried Wartle.

But Grace did not have hands. She stamped back and forth on the bank, worrying about what to do.

That's when the kelpies came.

Have you ever seen a kelpie? You wouldn't like it. And you'd like three kelpies even less. Which is unfortunate, because there were *three* of them.

Kelpies are nasty Fairy Creatures. They look like horses, if a horse's hair was greasy-gray and if a horse's mane was made of slimy green river plants. And if a horse swam in the water, waiting to grab anyone who came in so it could pull them under and drown them.

Because drowning folk is what kelpies did. Maybe they did it for food. Maybe they did it for fun. I really don't know. But Curious was in the river, and he was about to find out.

The good news was, he wouldn't have to be curious about kelpies anymore.

The bad news was, he wouldn't have to be curious about anything else. Ever. Again.

I know what you're thinking. If Curious drowns now, that'll be it for our story. Something's got to save him, right?

You may be thinking that. But you can look ahead and see how many chapters are left in this book. Whereas Curious, he doesn't even know he's in a book. So he's not thinking that at all. He's thinking that it's all over. He's done. He's fighting the kelpies off as best as he can, kicking in every direction. But it's hard to kick in the water, and they keep grabbing at his tail and his legs and pulling him under.

Each time they do, he gets a big mouthful of water, and then he has to struggle to reach air. He's gasping and sputtering. It doesn't look good.

Wartle is caught up in his mane, and he's looking very much like a drowning rat. His hands aren't doing him any good either.

Grace is running frantically back and forth on the bank. She's shouting unhelpfully and whinnying in fear. Any minute now her terror of the kelpies is going to outpace her loyalty to Curious, and she's going to buck and run.

And then where will Curious be?

Whatever you're thinking, it doesn't look good.

WAIT! HE CAN'T DIE NOW! WHAT WOULD THE REST OF THE BOOK BE ABOUT?

Down Curious went, under the water, for the third time! Maybe for the last time!

But just as he went under, Midnight burst from the Whisperwood with Vision at her heels.

"There it is," she said. She raised a hoof to point at the ghostly blue light bobbing over the River Restless. Vision followed her gaze. Then she snorted in shock.

"*That's* what you're after?" said Vision. "You do know that's a wispy wood wink, don't you?"

"Yes, of course I know," said Midnight.

"What does a wispy wood wink have to do with the Plan?" asked Vision.

"It's everything to do with the Plan," said Midnight. "It practically *is* the Plan. It's a ghost fire, right?"

"Yes," said Vision.

"But it's blue."

"Yes," said Vision.

"Our fire is red. Or orange. Mine is really red."

"So?"

"So I need to control my fire, don't I?"

"Yes, but—"

"So if I want to control my fire, maybe I can change it."

"Change it how?"

"By mixing it with blue fire!"

"How are you going to do that?"

Midnight gave a big horsey smile full of teeth. It was an "I'm so smart—wait until you hear this—I bet nobody has ever thought of something so clever" kind of smile.

"By eating it!" Midnight declared. "Isn't that just the most brilliant Plan in the whole wide world?"

Vision looked at the wispy wood wink, and she looked at Midnight. She did not think it was the most brilliant Plan in the whole wide world. She had her own idea about it.

"You are *insane*!" she said. "That's the stupidest, crazi-est, worst-iest Plan I've ever heard."

"Yeah." Midnight smiled. "I just have to wait for it to drift back to our side of the river."

"Weren't you listening?" started Vision. "What part of 'insane' did you think meant I was endorsing you?"

"Um," said Midnight. "The part where you got all excited and shouty? I didn't really hear what you were saying, but I liked your enthusiasm."

"That wasn't enthusiasm!" yelled Vision. And they would have kept on arguing, but then Curious broke the surface of the river. He burst up after a really long dunking, and they saw him, sputtering and gasping and kicking up a big spray of water. Then the three kelpies rose too, braying and neighing and moving in to grab him again.

"Hey," said Midnight, "what's that unicorn doing there? And those kelpies? Don't they know that wispy wood wink is mine?"

"I don't think they're after the wispy wood wink," said Vision.

"Oh," said Midnight. "They're drowning the unicorn."

"Yes," said Vision. "Why don't we watch?"

"Watch?" said Midnight. "But shouldn't we do something?"

Vision thought about it.

"It's almost over," she said. "The kelpies pretty much have things under control without us."

"No," said Midnight, shocked. "I meant, shouldn't we *help* somehow?"

"I guess we could kick rocks at him," Vision said.

"No. I mean help *him*."

"Help the unicorn?" Vision blinked. "What would we do that for?"

"Because he's drowning."

"I still don't follow you," said Vision.

"They're going to drown him."

"I'm with you there," said Vision.

"So we should help."

"Help. The. Unicorn." Vision said the words again as if she still couldn't understand what they meant. Then she looked at Midnight.

"But we *hate* unicorns. We *all* hate unicorns. We hate *all* unicorns. *I* hate unicorns. Don't *you* hate unicorns?"

"Of course I hate unicorns," said Midnight. Because she did. Automatically. She'd never given it a second thought. Hating unicorns was just what you did if you lived in the Whisperwood. All night mares hated unicorns. They were snooty and stuck-up and they chased night mares out of the best parts of the isle. They looked down their noses at you, and they never had you over for occasional marshmallow parties at the palace. That's why she hated unicorns.

But then she wondered, *Do I really?*

Do I really hate unicorns?

She realized she probably did. But hating unicorns in general and watching one die right in front of your eyes in what was very definitely not a fair fight were two different things.

"Think of it this way," said Vision. "It's one less unicorn in the world."

"You're right," said Midnight. "One less unicorn."

They watched the unicorn struggle.

"He is putting up quite a fight," said Midnight.

"Not one he can win," said Vision.

"Still . . ."

Vision let out a snort of disgust.

"Don't tell me you like him?"

"Hey," objected Midnight. "I hate the unicorns as much as anyone. More, even."

"Good," said Vision. "Because you know if it was you in the water, that unicorn would stand on the bank and laugh while you drowned."

"You're probably right," Midnight agreed.

"You know I am. They hate us."

"Yes, but they hate all the creatures of the Whisperwood."

"They hate night mares the most, though," said Vision. "It's like they think we're just the worst, like we're the evil opposite of unicorns."

"The evil opposite," repeated Midnight. She thought about those words. Evil. Opposite. Were the unicorns right? Was she the evil opposite of a unicorn?

She wasn't sure, but one thing she did know: An evil opposite wouldn't lift a hoof to save a unicorn.

The unicorn went underwater again.

"I don't think he's coming up this time," said Vision. "Good."

"I *do* hate unicorns," said Midnight.

"There you go," said Vision.

"You know what I hate most about them?" asked Midnight.

"Their horns?" said Vision.

"Nope."

"Their perfect coats?"

"Nope."

"Their silly names?"

"Nope."

"What, then?"

"I hate them for being so wrong about us."

She trotted forward to the bank of the River Restless.

"Hey!" shouted Vision. "Where are you going?"

"To prove we're better than they are," Midnight replied. "I'm no one's evil opposite."

And with that, Midnight plunged into the water.

☘ 4 ☘

ONE (NOT) EVIL OPPOSITE TO THE RESCUE

Midnight hit the water with a splash.

The River Restless was swift. It could pull a horse down easily, even without any kelpies doing its job for it. But Midnight was strong. She fought hard against the current.

With powerful strokes of her four legs, she soon reached the spot where the unicorn had vanished.

She dove.

Now, every bit of water in the Glistening Isles is always crystal clear. Bright as a mirror. Shining as a diamond.

Unless, of course, it's *supposed* to be spooky water, and then it's dark and murky, foul-smelling and bubbly. But the water of the River Restless was as transparent as glass. Rushing, dangerous, bracingly cold glass.

Midnight could see the unicorn below her. She saw the snarling kelpies biting at him. Three-on-one was not a fair fight. It made her angry. And that stoked her fires.

She kicked as hard as she could. The water slowed her down, but she put her all into it. *Thwump!*

The kelpie's hide was squishy and slimy. It felt like stomping on a fish. By itself, Midnight's kick wasn't much. But when she struck kelpie scales, a burst of flame shot out of her hoof. It made the water boil and sent up a cloud of hot bubbles.

"Ow, ow, ow!" yelped the kelpie. "What'd you go and do that for?"

Kelpies can talk underwater. I don't know how, but they can. You can hear everything they say to you just like they were whispering in your ear. Of course, few people know this, because very few people who hear a kelpie speaking under the water ever come back up to talk about it.

Midnight couldn't talk underwater, but she wasn't interested in talking. She was there to fight. She struck the next kelpie the same way. A swift kick. A gout of fire. Steam and bubbles.

"Ow, ow, ow!" it yelped. "That was mean!"

Midnight attacked the third kelpie.

But the third kelpie was determined. It was tenacious. It was unshakable. It wouldn't let go of the unicorn. Not when it almost had him.

That was a problem. But Midnight realized she just had to try harder. She just needed to give the kelpie more motivation.

She swam closer. She opened her mouth. Then she bit down on the kelpie's flank hard. She nearly gagged on the nasty fish taste. But she didn't.

Instead, she blew the hottest blast of flame she could muster. The fires squirted out between her strong teeth.

Now there was a taste in her mouth like sizzling salmon.

"Yeeee-ow!" the kelpie yelled. It bucked, it twisted, and it twirled. It was trying to dislodge her. But Midnight refused to let go until it did.

It sizzled some more. It let go.

All three kelpies swam away from her. They hung back, watching and nursing their wounds.

But the unicorn was starting to sink.

Midnight dove deeper. She wasn't going to let the stupid unicorn go and drown now. Not when she'd fought off three kelpies for him. He needed to live. He needed to see how much better she was than him. How she wasn't his evil opposite. She clamped her teeth on his mane and tugged.

He was heavy. Like dead weight.

Don't give up now, you dumb unicorn, Midnight thought.

She pulled and pulled and pulled.

Finally, they broke through the surface of the River Restless and into the air. For a moment, all either of them could do was snort and wheeze, wheeze and snort.

And then the unicorn looked at her.

"You—you saved me?" he said. "Why?"

"That's a good question," said one of the kelpies. Midnight saw that they were coming closer again. "This unicorn was ours. If you want one, you should go get your own."

"I don't want my own," said Midnight. "I don't want any unicorns."

"Oh," said the kelpie. "No, of course you don't. You must have thought he was something else. A big fish maybe. If it was a misunderstanding, well, no problem. We'll take it from here."

All three kelpies began to swim toward the unicorn again.

"No, no!" cried Midnight. "You can't have him either."

"I don't understand," said a kelpie. "If you don't want him, we do. Either you drown him or we will."

"No one is drowning anyone," said Midnight.

"I don't see how that makes any sense," said a kelpie. "Drowning folks is what kelpies do."

"Well," growled Midnight, "you'll drown this unicorn over my dead body."

"Then it's settled," the kelpie said brightly. "I'm glad we could come to an arrangement. We drown you both."

"That's not what I meant," objected Midnight, but the kelpies weren't listening. Now that they understood the situation they were back on mission.

Curious cast a panicked look at Midnight.

"What do we do?" he asked.

"I use my fire," said Midnight.

"And what do I do?" said Curious.

"You? You go back down." And with that, Midnight reached out a hoof and shoved Curious under the water.

Then she thought the angriest, wildest thought she could think, and flames shot from her mouth and flew from her nostrils and even spurted from her ears. The kelpies all reared back, their nasty green plant-hair singed and burning.

Curious came right up, sputtering. He saw the smoke and the burned kelpie hair and his eyes went wide.

"Can you swim?" Midnight yelled at him.

Curious didn't have enough breath to answer, but he nodded vigorously.

"Then swim!" yelled Midnight.

She took off through the water, heading for her side of the bank. But the current was strong, and the kelpies were blocking her way. And they were very angry.

The opposite bank was nearer.

There wasn't time to think about it.

She had no choice.

She had to swim . . .

To the unicorn side.

Midnight turned and swam, Curious behind her.

The kelpies snatched at them, but they reached the bank. They climbed onto the shore, panting, gasping, spitting water from their mouths.

"Come back here and drown like you're supposed to!" shouted the kelpies. Then they shouted some rude and angry words at them. They told the horses that they were mean and unfair and they called them nasty names, but Midnight and Curious stayed well away from the riverbank. Finally, the monsters sunk below the waters. Midnight could see them down there, blowing angry bubbles and sulking.

Then she turned her attention to the unicorn.

Midnight could see the water running off his hide in rivulets. And the mud from the riverbank was drying and flaking off his legs. He'd be spotless in a minute. Whereas she was wet and muddy. She blew a disgusted breath. Of course unicorns would be self-cleaning! It was so exasperating!

"Curious," he said.

"About what?" Midnight snapped.

"No, I mean I'm Curious. I mean my name is Curious."

"What do I want to know your name for?"

The unicorn looked stunned.

"But—but you just saved me."

"So?" said Midnight. She shook her mane vigorously. Water droplets flew off and spattered the unicorn, but they started evaporating immediately.

"I don't understand why you would do it," said Curious. Then he narrowed his eyes and stared at her. "Does that mean I'm in your power now or something?"

"What?"

"Do I owe you a life debt? Did you save my life so that I would have to be your zombie thrall?" He twisted his neck, trying to examine himself from hooves to tail.

"I don't feel much like a zombie," he said. "I'm pretty much still me. Are you sure you did it correctly?"

"You're not my zombie," snorted Midnight.

"Then you were trying to take me prisoner," Curious pronounced. "Only we came out on the wrong side of the river."

"I wasn't taking you prisoner."

"Not very well, obviously."

"You're not my prisoner. You're not my thrall. You're not my zombie."

"Hmm," said Curious. "Are you sure you're a proper night mare?"

He leaned in close, trying to study Midnight's muzzle. She snorted out a little burst of fire that made him rear back swiftly.

"Okay, you're a night mare," he said. "But you're a strange one. Don't worry, though. I'll figure it out. I have a Scientific Mind."

"That's right," said Wartle, suddenly emerging from where he had been tangled up in Curious's mane this entire time. "He has a Scientific Mind."

Midnight reared in surprise.

"What is that?"

"That's Wartle," said Curious.

"What's a wartle doing in your mane?"

"He's a puckle, not a wartle. His *name* is Wartle."

Midnight peered at the furry little creature. She had heard of puckles but never met one. She only met the nastier sort of fairy in the Whisperwood.

"That still doesn't explain what he was doing in your mane," she said.

"He's my friend," said Curious. "Also, he helps me with things."

"Helps?"

"Hands," said Wartle. He held up his pink fingers and wriggled them proudly.

"Very useful when conducting experiments," said Curious.

"I suppose," said Midnight. She didn't know what an experiment was, but she certainly wasn't going to admit to it. "Still, it doesn't seem very unicorny to keep a wartle in your mane."

"A puckle. His name is Wartle."

"But, isn't he a little, well, funny-looking for a unicorn to wear?"

"Funny-looking!" objected Wartle.

"Sorry," said Midnight. "But everyone knows unicorns can't stand anything that's not as beautiful as they think they are."

"Ha," said Curious. "That shows what you know. I am a unicorn with a Scientific Mind. I want to understand important things. I want to glean their inner workings. I don't just gawk at something because it's pretty."

"I am pretty," said Wartle in a little, hurt voice. "Inner workings and all."

Midnight let out a long whinny of a laugh. She wasn't

laughing at Wartle. That would be mean. She was laughing at Curious.

"Whoever heard of a unicorn with a Scientific Mind? That's the dumbest thing I've ever heard. Unicorns don't have minds. Their heads don't have room for anything else besides their own giant egos."

Curious stamped a hoof angrily.

"Not true," he said. "You only think that because you're a Creature of Wickedness."

"I am not a Creature of Wickedness!" Midnight objected.

"You live in the Whisperwood, don't you?" said Curious.

"Well, yes."

"And Wicked Creatures live in the Whisperwood, don't they?"

"Well, yes, but—"

"Then it follows that you are a Creature of Wickedness. If you don't understand this, it is because you don't have a Scientific Mind, but trust me, it all makes sense when you have an enlightened perspective."

"Look, idiot," said Midnight, "if I'm a Creature of Wickedness, then what did I save you for? Explain that, huh?"

Curious was silent a moment. Then he mumbled something.

"What's that?" asked Midnight.

"I can't explain it," Curious repeated. "It's inexplicable."

"Inexplicable," repeated Wartle.

Curious sighed. Then he brightened. He was never down for long.

"There must be something wrong with you. You must be broken in some way. You are malfunctioning."

"Malfunctioning?"

"I don't know how, but don't worry, I'll figure it out."

"You don't have to figure it out," said Midnight. "I'll tell you. I saved you because we night mares are better than you unicorns."

"Horsefeathers!" said Curious. This was a horsey expression. It meant something was ridiculous and impossible. Because, obviously, horses didn't have feathers.

(Obviously, the unicorns of the Glistening Isles had never met a hippalectryon or a pegasus, or they would know there are at least two horses that do have feathers. Though, admittedly, one of them is ridiculous and the other is impossible.)

"We are better!" insisted Midnight.

"You are not," said Curious. He was really offended now. Which wasn't something his Scientific Mind was prepared for.

"We are. And I proved it by rescuing you."

"That doesn't prove anything."

"It does."

"It does," said Wartle. Then the puckle realized he was repeating for the other side. He wiggled his fingers again to remind Curious of their usefulness.

And speaking of the other side, what do you think happened to Midnight's friend Vision? She was on the opposite bank of the River Restless. She saw Midnight rescue the unicorn, but she couldn't believe it. When Midnight swam to the unicorn side of the river, she *really* couldn't believe it. But what she *really, really* couldn't believe was that her friend was talking—*talking!*—with the unicorn now. She couldn't *believe* it, but that didn't mean she was going to *stand* for it.

"Hey, Midnight?" she yelled. And she yelled it over and over, getting louder and louder. "Midnight! Midniiiiiiight!"

Curious and Midnight finally heard her. The unicorn looked across the waters to the fiery horse on the shore.

"What is that night mare doing telling us the time?" he asked.

"She's not telling us the time," said Midnight.

"She seems awfully interested that we know it."

"She's not telling us the time!"

"Midnight!" Vision hollered.

"There she goes again," said Curious.

"Midnight, get back here!" Vision shouted.

"I can't," said Midnight. "I'm stuck."

"Oh, I get it," said Curious. "Your name is *Midnight*."

"Great," said Midnight. "Now the unicorn knows my name."

"Yes," said Curious. He gave Midnight a smug expression. "And I must say, it's a fitting name for a Creature of Wickedness."

"For the last time," snarled Midnight, "I. AM. NOT. A. CREATURE. OF. WICKEDNESS."

Of course, she was so mad that flames shot out of her mouth. And nose. And ears. And probably her bottom too if you want to be indelicate but accurate. They scorched the grass all around her in a circle and sent up a puff of black smoke.

Midnight stood in a circle of ash, panting and glowering angrily, her eyes blazing red and little dark clouds rising into the air around her.

Curious gave Midnight a very skeptical look.

"I think we'll have to agree to disagree," he said.

Before Midnight could respond, Wartle interrupted.

"Winky!" he cried. Then he used his hands to point at the wispy wood wink, which had drifted back over the land and was slinking off into the woods.

"Winky," Wartle cried again.

"My wispy wood wink!" said Curious.

"It's *my* wispy wood wink!" replied Midnight. "And it's getting away!"

"Yours?" said Curious. "It's not yours; it's mine!"

"Only if you catch it first," said Midnight. Then she burst into a gallop.

"Hey! What—wait!" Curious stammered. Then he broke into a run as well.

And just like that, the chase was on.

5

WHAT'S THAT BRIDGE DOING THERE?

The wispy wood wink was bobbing furiously. It flew through the air, floating parallel to the river. Its glowing blue light was getting smaller and smaller as it flew farther and farther.

"It can't get away!" yelled Midnight. "I have to eat it!"

She kicked up her hooves and redoubled her charge.

Curious almost stumbled at her words. Surely he hadn't heard her correctly.

"*Eat* it?" the unicorn cried. "What do you mean '*eat* it'? You can't *eat* it! It's for my Experiment."

And he, too, kicked up his hooves, and he charged after Midnight.

"Hands!" shouted Wartle, clinging tightly onto Curious's back. He didn't have hooves to kick. And he didn't quite follow what was happening, so he thought it was a good idea to remind everyone again why he was special.

The two horses raced along the riverbank, the puckle clinging to one of them.

Midnight was fast. But Curious was desperate.

He was hot on her heels. Which was impressive, because her heels were hot.

Little fires flared where she stepped. They burned out quickly in her wake, but Curious had to watch where he put a hoof or—

"Ow, ow, ow!" he yelped whenever he stepped on her flaming hoofprints. "That burns!"

"Then stop following me!" Midnight shouted.

"I'm not following you. I'm following my wispy wood wink!"

"You mean *my* wispy wood wink," replied Midnight. "I've been after it all night. I'm going to eat it."

"Oh, no," said Curious. "That's *my* wood wink. I've been after it all night. And eating it is *not* part of the

Experiment. Catching it, yes. Studying it, yes. Eating it, no!"

"Don't eat Winky!" yelled Wartle.

Yes, they were quite a sight.

But they weren't the only sight to see.

Not at all.

Because up ahead, just a little ways farther up the river, there was a Something that was very, very out of place on the Glistening Isles.

The wispy wood wink paused in its flight. Then it turned at a right angle and dove into the shelter of this new, strange Something.

Both unicorn and night mare stopped short.

"What is that?" said Midnight. She was suspicious of this new Something.

"I don't know," said Curious. He was just as suspicious as she was, but he remembered that he was not just a unicorn, but also a scientist. He had to act a certain way. "But my Scientific Mind will investigate," he proclaimed, trying to sound braver than he felt.

He trotted forward.

The Something, whatever it was, was made of old and rotting planks of wood. It had moss growing on it in spots, and holes in other spots where bits of it had crumbled away with age. That was very weird, because nothing built of fairy magic could ever age and rot and crumble away on the Glistening Isles.

"Bridge," said Puckle.

"What?" said both horses.

"It's a covered bridge," replied the little fairy. "For going across the river." He demonstrated by making four of his fingers walk across his palm. Then, amused with himself, he made his fingers dance a jig.

"But why does it look like that?" said Midnight. "This isn't a fairy bridge, is it?"

"I don't think it is," said Curious. "If the queen made a bridge, it would be a big shining hunk of clear crystal. Or a rainbow maybe. Or a path of yellow bricks."

"And I'm pretty sure any Wicked Fairy would make a bridge of black stones and frozen smoke," said Midnight. "Or solid fire. Or a storm cloud. It might be scary, but it wouldn't look so worn and, well, sad as this one does. Who builds a bridge out of old wood, anyway?"

"I think it's human-made," said Curious.

"Impossible," said Midnight.

"To the enlightened mind, nothing is impossible," said Curious. He said it because he thought it sounded impressive, though in truth he didn't actually know what it meant.

"Do you think it's from long ago?" asked Midnight. "I mean, from before."

She meant from the time before the fairies came to the Glistening Isles, when these islands had been home to some very wild and blue-tattooed humans. But everything from that time was all gone.

All, it seemed, except for this lone, sad, rotting little bridge.

"Wow," said Midnight.

"Wow," said Curious.

And Wartle would have said "wow" too, only then Something new happened upon them.

For a moment, neither Curious nor Midnight could speak. They were too busy staring, mouths hanging open, at the Something coming at them.

Remember that pumpkin that was watching our night mares, Vision and Midnight? And you wondered how a pumpkin could watch anyone?

Well, this is how.

Picture a person. Or at least something that walks on two legs and has two arms and is dressed like a person, although its clothes are shabby and tattered. And its head . . . well, that head is very definitely *not* like a person. Not like a person at all.

Because you see as it approaches . . .

The head is a *pumpkin.* A great orange jack-o'-lantern. With a toothy grin. A triangle hole for nose. And two wicked eyes sliced into its shell. And out of those two wicked eyes the flickering yellow light of a candle flame shines.

This, my friends, is Jack o' the Hunt.

Doesn't his very name make you shiver and shake and cry for Daddy?

Brrrr . . .

Jack o' the Hunt is a Wicked Fairy. Maybe the worst Wicked Fairy on the Glistening Isles. It's hard to know for sure, because the others mostly stay in their Dark Castle. But Jack o' the Hunt doesn't stay put. He roams the land. He wanders hither, thither, and yon.

He's a member of the Court of Thistles. Or maybe the messenger of the Court of Thistles. Or maybe he's the Court Jester.

There are those who say he is all those things. And there are those who say that Jack serves only himself. They say if the Court of Thistles thinks Jack works for them, that's only because Jack has fooled them good.

What do I think? I think if you ever see Jack coming you should head the other way. That's what I think.

Because whatever Jack is, he's bee-ay-dee bad!

So head the other way.

Unfortunately, at least for one of our horses, heading the other way meant going across the bridge.

To the other side of the river.

To night mare territory.

And you know which horse didn't want to do that.

Righto. Our unicorn.

Curious had never been on that side of the river in all his young life, and he didn't plan to go there now.

But his Scientific Mind was rapidly coming up short of other options. So he tore his eyes from Jack and glanced at the bridge.

The bridge might not be as sturdy as he'd like, but it did stretch across the River Restless. And most of its boards were still in place, even if they were rotten and full of holes.

So maybe he wouldn't fall in if he walked across. The nonscientific parts of his mind cried out, then you'll be on the *other side*. And that might be *worse.*

Jack spoke. His pumpkin head didn't have a tongue, so I don't know how he spoke. But speak he did.

Jack's tongueless mouth spoke in a deep voice. He sounded like he was very pleased with himself. Like he found everything a little bit funny.

Also, he spoke in rhyme.

(Rhyming fairies are the worst!)

And this is what he said.

"What is this, that Jack does spy
With his hollow pumpkin eye?

The Thistle Court would say Jack lied
To tell of unicorn 'n' night mare side by side."

At those last words, Midnight snapped out of her fright. Truth told, she was never very frightened of anything. Not for long. Cold fear wasn't a match for hot fire. The fire inside her always burned up all her fear before it could really catch hold.

"I'm not *with* the unicorn," Midnight sneered. "We just so happen to be chasing after the same thing, that's all."

Winky must have understood some of that, because the blue light shining out from the covered bridge suddenly flickered as if in panic.

Jack's candle flames wavered. Was he looking over the horses at the wispy wood wink? What would a pumpkin-headed fairy want with a wood wink? It wasn't very likely that a pumpkin had a Scientific Mind like Curious. Jack's mouth was just a carved hole in a shell, so it's doubtful he wanted to eat the wink like Midnight. And it's hard to be sure where a candle flame looks. When Jack spoke again, his voice had a wistful note.

"Oh, how I long to ride this unicorn!
But alas, alack, Jack's so forlorn.

The queen's anger he'll not dare.
Perhaps the Flower Court would share?"

Now it was Curious's turn to be offended by Jack's verse. He didn't like the tone of Jack's words at all. No one rode unicorns. No one! Except *maybe* the fairy queen. And that was only because they *let* her—because she had done so much for them, and she didn't weigh very much at all. Curious certainly wasn't someone's toy pony to be shared about with Wicked Fairy Creatures.

"We're not her mounts; we're not her pets," he said, glaring at the grinning pumpkin. "We're her friends." Unfortunately, this only made Jack o' the Hunt laugh—Ho ho he he ho—and then he sang another rhyme.

"Why, you've all the freedom of a rose
That outside palace window grows!
One day she'll spy you on her lawn,
And pluck at dusk what blooms at dawn."

"We belong only to ourselves," insisted Curious. But Jack's words were making him curiously uncomfortable. Because he couldn't help but wonder just what Jack meant. He didn't get very far in his thinking, though, because just then Midnight interrupted him.

"Hey, unicorn," she said. "Maybe now's not the right time to press that point. Jack won't take you if he thinks you have the queen's protection."

The pumpkin head bobbed in sad agreement.

"The little black filly's words are very true,
But enough talk, Jack has things to do."

Then the Wicked Fairy raised his hands, which were wrapped in tattered gloves to match his threadbare clothes, and his long fingers twisted strangely in the air in uncomfortable ways. To Midnight and Curious, it looked like he was casting magic spells. Which, of course, he was.

Shoop! Shoop! Shoop!

Pumpkin vines sprouted from the ground around our horses' hooves. They grew up into the air. They writhed like evil green snakes. They reached their leafy tendrils for the horses' unprotected legs.

"Look out!" shouted Midnight, though it was a rather obvious thing to say. She reared away from the vines, little flames bursting from her nostrils in anger. Then she backed up the ramp and into the shelter of the bridge.

Curious hesitated. He didn't want to follow. Wicked Fairies were on the other side. And that was a good point.

But, his Scientific Mind argued, the wickedest of them all was right here. And that was a better point.

He ripped his legs free of the grasping pumpkin plants and ran to join Midnight.

They stood together under the shelter of the rooftop covering, watching as Jack advanced.

"Come on," Midnight said, beginning to move backward across the bridge. Even as she spoke, Midnight was wondering why she was waiting for the unicorn. It's not like she was *with* him. And he certainly wasn't her *responsibility.*

"But . . . ," said Curious. "That's your side."

"So?"

"So, I'm a unicorn."

Midnight almost said "So?" again. But she realized that Curious was right to be afraid. Even if she wasn't a threat to him, she couldn't say the same for her herd. And she was absolutely certain there were fairies and Fairy Creatures who would love to eat a unicorn. Curious wouldn't be safe on her side of the River Restless. He'd have to stand and fight Jack here. Midnight could leave him to do it, but then Curious would be dead, and then who would tell all the other unicorns about how much better a night mare was than them?

She shook her mane in disgust at the way her evening was going.

"Don't tell me I'm going to have to save you again?" Midnight snorted.

"Save me?"

Midnight shouldered her way beside him on the bridge.

"We can make our stand here and fight."

"Okay," said Curious. "But maybe I'm saving *you*! Did you think of that?"

"No," Midnight replied. "I did not."

And then they didn't really have time to talk, because Jack was upon them. And their fight began.

※ 6 ※
AND THEN SOMETHING PRETTY BAD HAPPENS

Huge green tendrils writhed all around Jack o' the Hunt. They seemed more like the tentacles of a sea monster than the vines of a plant. They reached over Jack's shoulders and slithered around Jack's legs to grasp at the horses.

Curious and Midnight reared and dodged. Still the tendrils came.

They reared and dodged some more. They reared and dodged a lot.

That's when they noticed something.

The vines kept falling short.

The plants were certainly long enough to reach them. They were certainly quick enough to catch them, strong enough to pull them.

But a vine would stretch out, almost gripping one or the other of them, and then, suddenly, it would recoil.

Almost as if it hit something. Like a fence. Or a window, or an invisible wall.

Which was really odd, really strange, and for a certain pumpkin really *frustrating.*

Jack scowled. He couldn't understand what was happening either. He turned his pumpkin head all around, back and forth, and then . . . upward.

Curious followed Jack's gaze. As I said before, it was hard to know where a pumpkin was looking. But there wasn't anything at all that Curious could see.

Just an odd small thing, a curved bit of metal nailed into the gable of the bridge. If you saw the odd metal thing, you would say that it was shaped like the letter U. But Curious didn't know how to read. Curious just thought of it as a funny-shaped thing, and probably a rock, because, of course, the Glistening Isles didn't have any metal on them either. Or not much. So he didn't know what it was or what it was made of. But you, I'll bet, know exactly what it was.

It was a horseshoe, nailed for luck over the top of the covered bridge.

A horseshoe.

Now that's a pretty common thing in the rest of the world. And in your world, too, I'm sure.

But not here, not on the Glistening Isles, where no one ever, ever shoes a horse.

So it must have been something held over from long ago, when those wild and blue-tattooed humans lived in these isles, before the fairies came.

That's something to think about later. Because right now things are about to get worse.

Because Jack wasn't a fairy to give up what he wanted.

Oh, no! Jack was a fairy to get what he wanted.

And right now, he wanted those two horses.

Didn't he?

He must have. Because when he saw that his vines weren't reaching them, he tried something else.

Suddenly, little orange orbs started sprouting all over his vines.

They swelled up like balloons (though, of course, Curious and Midnight didn't know what balloons were either).

They grew ripe and plump and fat.

They were pumpkins! Dozens of pumpkins!

Jack hurled them. He slung them through the air like missiles.

And they could get through the invisible wall.

Maybe because they were flying so fast.

They burst like pulpy orange bombs on our horses.

They struck the walls of the bridge.

They caused the whole covered bridge to shake and tremble.

And then, as the bridge shuddered, that horseshoe came loose from its nail.

And fell.

Have you ever played horseshoes? Have you ever tossed them at a pole?

Well, it was like that.

The horseshoe dropped straight down, and it caught on Curious's horn.

He shook his head, hoping to dislodge it.

But that only spun the horseshoe round and round.

And as it spun, Jack seemed to stumble.

The bad rhyming fairy looked dizzy. Confused.

This was very interesting to Curious and his Scientific Mind, and he would have considered it further.

But then the bridge collapsed.

All the rearing and stamping and hurling of pumpkins was too much for the poor old thing.

The supports under it snapped.

The whole bridge, covered roof and all, collapsed into the River Restless.

This surprised everyone.

Curious. Midnight. Wartle, who had been hiding in Curious's mane. It surprised Jack. It probably even surprised Winky.

Jack's carved pumpkin eyes widened across his shell.

And then our horses were spinning round and round as the covered bridge was swept away in the swift currents of the River Restless.

They were being carried far away from Jack.

On the one hoof, that was a good thing.

But on the other hoof, now they were in danger from the river itself.

They stumbled back and forth, as floorboards broke away beneath them.

The whole bridge shuddered and groaned as the river began rapidly to tear it apart.

Curious and Midnight ran back and forth, trying to stay on their hooves and not go down with the bridge.

But the bridge was spinning really fast. Crashing into rocks. Tumbling over waterfalls. Swirling round and round and round.

And then suddenly, for one hopeful instant, they saw a bank just a few feet away. Was it the unicorn side? Was it the night mare side? It didn't matter. They had only seconds.

"Jump!" they both yelled at each other.

They jumped.

And they landed.

Whump!

Behind them, the whole bridge shuddered and shook and collapsed into the waters.

And then it was gone.

"That was close," Curious said, which was an obvious thing to say.

"Yes, it was," said Midnight, because she was being obvious too.

"Close, close, close," said Wartle, because he wanted to be included.

Then they all did the next obvious thing, which was to see which side of the river they were on.

If they were on the unicorn side, Midnight would be in trouble. And if they were on the night mare side, Curious would be in trouble.

Wartle would be fine either way. He could always slip into one of the smaller fairy doors. And anyway, nobody much noticed puckles.

As to Winky, who knew what a wispy wood wink thought about trouble, if it thought at all.

"Whisperwood," said Wartle. He pointed with a finger at the twisted, stunted, blackened trees that seemed to reach for them just a few feet away from the riverbank.

"Oh, no," said Curious.

"Oh, yes," said Midnight.

"But now I'm in real trouble," said Curious.

"Not immediately, you're not," said Midnight. "Which means I can say something I've wanted to say since I met you."

"What's that?" he asked.

"Good-bye," she replied.

And with that, Midnight began to trot away.

"You're leaving?" shouted Curious.

"That's what usually follows a 'good-bye,'" replied Midnight.

"You can't just leave me!" insisted Curious.

"Can. Am. Did," said Midnight.

"But what will happen to me?"

Midnight stopped. She blew an exasperated breath through her nostrils.

"I already saved you twice, unicorn. I don't *plan* to make a habit of it."

"But I don't know how to get back."

"That's certainly a problem," said Midnight. "But it isn't one of mine."

"Please," said Curious. "Help me."

"Why should I?" asked Midnight. "When has a unicorn ever helped a night mare?"

Curious was silent because the answer was "never." No unicorn had ever helped a night mare.

Midnight felt a little stab of guilt. She tried to brighten him up.

"Look," she said, "I'm sure you could find your way back if you'd just use that Scientific Mind of yours."

Curious was awfully proud of his Scientific Mind.

"Hmmm . . . ," he said. "I just might."

"There," said Midnight. "You see. I'm sure you'll work something out." She turned to go. She had things to do. Now, where had that wispy wood wink gotten to?

"Looking for this?" called Curious.

Midnight stopped.

She turned around.

Wartle was standing atop Curious's head. He was waving the Absorbing Orb. And it was now glowing with a new, blue light.

"My wink!" roared Midnight.

She galloped back to Curious.

"Give it here!" she roared.

She lunged for it, but Wartle leapt off of Curious and onto the ground.

Midnight dove at the puckle.

But Wartle ducked behind a rock. And when she kicked it over, he was gone.

Then he waved to her from the trunk of a tree.

"Not fair!" she cried. "He's using fairy doors!"

It was true. Wartle was running in and out of the little holes, ducking in and out of Elsewhither. The holes were too small for the bigger fairies, too small for unicorns and nightmares, but they were fine for little puckles.

Midnight chased him back and forth. He popped out of mushrooms and mudbanks and rocks. Each time he waved his hands at her merrily and then—*poof*—he disappeared again.

"This isn't fair!" yelled Midnight.

"Ah, but it is," said Curious. "You told me to use my Scientific Mind, and this is what my Scientific Mind came up with."

"Tormenting night mares?"

"No. A trade."

"A trade? What do you mean?"

"You help me get to my side of the river," explained Curious. "And I give you the Absorbing Orb with the wispy wood wink inside."

Midnight glowered. She grumbled. She groused.

But in the end she had to say . . .

"Deal."

Of course, she launched herself at Wartle one more time. And of course she missed.

So she had to apologize and say "Deal" again.

Probably the first deal ever between a unicorn and a night mare.

"Now," she said when she had calmed down and flames had stopped spurting out her nose, "I think I know who can get you back across the river."

"You do?" said Curious.

"Yes," she said. "But before I take you, we have to go somewhere first. And you have to let me borrow the Absorbing Orb."

"Never trust a night mare," said Curious. "That's what they say. I'm not giving it to you until I'm safely back in unicorn territory."

"I didn't say 'give' it to me," said Midnight. "I said 'borrow' it. You let me *borrow* it, I take you *home,* you *give* it to me then."

"No deal," said Curious. But he was bluffing.

"Then you can stay here forever for all I care," said Midnight. "Because if I can't borrow the Absorbing Orb now, then I don't need it at all later." And she wasn't bluffing. Because she really did need to be somewhere. And very soon. And the unicorn could see it in her oh-so-determined eyes.

Curious glowered. He grumbled. He groused.

But in the end he had to say . . .

"Deal."

🌿 7 🌿

A SCARY LITTLE ASIDE (SKIP THIS CHAPTER IF YOU'RE EASILY FRIGHTENED)

Now we're going to leave Curious and Midnight for a moment.

They've just been through an ordeal, so maybe they need a bit of a break.

They aren't getting one. They are in rather a hurry. Or Midnight is at least. And Curious is in a panic.

But we're still going to leave them alone for a page or two.

Because, you see, something else important is happening somewhere else, and we need to know what it is.

Now, do you remember Grace? She was Curious's friend.
Whatever happened to her?

As it turns out, she did buck and run when Curious went under the water.

Don't be too harsh on her.

Yes, she deserted her friend.

But she wasn't very brave. And she wasn't a swimmer.

And she was pretty upset about everything she saw.

Anyway, she was running for help.

To the queen probably. She would know what to do.

So she was maybe running on three parts fear and one part going for help.

Which can make anyone run really, really fast.

Only, as she ran, her legs kept getting tripped up on vines.

That was odd, because all the lands on the good fairy side of the River Restless were extremely well-manicured.

There were no brambles, no weeds, no undergrowth at all to trip a horse's hooves or snag a fairy's foot.

Nonetheless, she was tripping.

She looked down and she saw . . .

Pumpkin vines. Big green pumpkin vines.

And they weren't just lying there getting in her way.

They were moving!

They were slithering around like snakes. Almost like they were trying to ensnare her hooves on purpose.

And then they did ensnare her hooves.

And she had to stop.

And there, right in front of her, was a pumpkin.

With a face.

And it stood up.

And it spoke.

"Oh, what beauty! Oh, what grace!
So good to meet you face to face.
The prize Jack sought has run away,
So he'll cheer himself with other prey."

And then the vines were snaking up her legs. They were winding around her flank. They were wrapping around her neck.

And, lastly, and most frighteningly of all, they were twisting around her horn!

⚘ 8 ⚘

A FURY OF FESTERLINGS

"So there's good news and bad news," said Midnight.

The unicorn and the night mare were walking along the edge of the forest, heading upstream along the River Restless. They hadn't entered the wood yet.

"Bad news?" said Curious. Somehow this didn't surprise him. He didn't trust the night mare—why would he?

"The bad news," said Midnight, and she gave an embarrassed neigh, "is that when we were bobbing down the river on that old bridge, we were carried downstream away from my part of the Whisperwood. So we're farther away from where I need to be."

"Why is that bad?" asked Curious.

"I'm in a hurry," explained Midnight.

"And the good news?" said Curious.

"The good news is that I know a shortcut."

"I see," said Curious. So far none of this was very alarming.

"But there's more bad news," said Midnight.

Curious sighed. Of course there was.

"Which is what?" he asked.

"The more bad news is that the shortcut is through the Festering Fens."

"That sounds terrible," said Curious. He didn't know what the Festering Fens were, but they didn't sound very appealing.

"Oh, but there's more good news too," said Midnight. "The more good news is that there's a path through the Fens that is . . . *mostly* safe."

" 'Mostly safe' doesn't sound very safe at all," said Curious. "I don't think I want to go anywhere called the Festering Fens."

"That's just its name."

"It's not a very welcoming one."

"Well, no," agreed Midnight. "The fens are yucky and mucky, it's true. But it's a *short*cut. That means we don't have to be in the fens for very *long.* And we'll get where we're going on time."

"Which is where?"

"Where I need to be."

"Which is *where*?"

As you might imagine, our ponies are going to go on like this for a while. But Midnight is going to win the argument in the end, because Curious doesn't really have a choice other than to go along with her if he wants to get home. So she's going to lead him through the Festering Fens despite his complaints. So while they argue about it pointlessly, let me ask you something with a point.

Do you know what you call a herd of unicorns?

Well, I guess you call them a herd, sure. But lots of creatures come in herds. Cows and cats and children, I suppose. Shouldn't there be another term for a gathering of creatures as magnificent as unicorns?

Well, there is.

In fact, nearly every animal—or at least every *interesting* animal—has a name for a group of a whole bunch of them together.

So you have an army of ants. A swarm of bees. A colony of beavers. A murder of crows. Nice one, that. A school of fish. An embarrassment of pandas. A pod of whales. A wisdom of wombats.

And magical creatures are no different. They need

fancy-schmancy names for when they all congregate too. So what do you call a lot of unicorns together?

You call them a *Blessing.*

A Blessing of unicorns.

That's what they are. It tells you right off how special they think they are, to call themselves a Blessing.

And so, of course, what do you think a herd of night mares is called?

It's going to be the opposite of a Blessing, isn't it?

It sure is.

So what's the evil opposite of a Blessing?

A *Curse.*

A Curse of night mares.

Not very nice. Not very fair. But there you go.

A Curse of night mares.

Why do I mention this now?

Well, for two reasons, really.

One is that the Curse is where Midnight is heading. Where she needs to be. And she needs to be there *by midnight.*

Clocks aren't important on the Glistening Isles, sure, but every night mare knows when midnight is. And midnight is important.

And the other reason why I told you about Blessings and Curses? Well, the other reason will become important shortly. But right now, let's catch up with Midnight and Curious.

I see that they're still arguing.

"I can't go to *the Curse*!" Curious yelped. And he was right. He couldn't go. Not if he didn't want to be torn to pieces.

"I'm not asking you to!" Midnight yelled back.

"But you're going," Curious pointed out.

"That's right."

"And I'm with you."

Midnight sighed.

"We've been through this before. You are not *with* me, unicorn."

Curious rethought his words.

"I am traveling *alongside* you, then," he suggested.

"*Alongside,* but not *with.*"

"And that means if you go to the Curse, I'll be *alongside* it too."

Midnight snorted.

"Don't worry," she said. "I have a Plan."

"Will you tell me what it is?"

Midnight shook her head.

"Past experience has taught me that it's best if only I know my Plans. Other horses don't seem to get my Plans when I explain them beforehoof."

"Your Plans sound like my Experiments," said Curious.

"It's nothing like those," objected Midnight. "I'm sure I don't do Experiments. Anyway, trust me, you don't want to hear my Plan."

Curious was usually not on this side of a conversation about *doing something dangerous.* But he did have past experience with telling someone they didn't want to hear something.

"That means I really *do* want to hear it," he said.

"I said you didn't."

"If I didn't, then I do. If I did, then I wouldn't need to."

Midnight was about to object, or at least to try to untangle that mess of words, but she was interrupted.

You see, they were working their way through a barely noticeable path that meandered through the Festering Fens, which were every bit as yucky and mucky as you might imagine. And the yucky, mucky path had been winding its way toward the Silent Stones, where the Curse spent each night.

Unfortunately, Midnight and Curious hadn't been particularly quiet.

They hadn't been particularly careful.

The Festering Fens of the Whisperwood were no place for that. No place at all.

Because you could attract all sorts of unwanted attention if you weren't quiet and careful.

And they weren't. And they did.

"Ow," said Curious. He suddenly stumbled. "Ow, ow, ow."

"What is it?" said Midnight.

"A pain in my knee," he said.

"Your knee?"

"Yes. Right, front."

Midnight grunted. She was in a hurry and pains in the knee weren't that serious. What did she care if the unicorn had a pain in his knee?

"This is odd," Curious said.

"Why?" said Midnight. "Are you going to tell me that unicorns never get knee pains?"

"Well, we don't," said Curious. "Our horns heal everything."

"Oh," said Midnight. That irritated her. Then she remembered where they were. And why they were called the Festering Fens. And maybe why her shortcut wasn't such a good idea after all. So she stopped walking and bent her neck to examine Curious's knee.

It was scraped. And looking all oozy and puffy and gross.

Curious saw it too. His eyes went wide. He'd never had any sort of infection before, so his reaction was a lot bigger than it needed to be.

"I'm dyyyyyyyyying!" he shouted.

"You're not dying," Midnight chided him.

"Yes, I am, I'm dying! Here in the Whisperwood with only a Creature of Wickedness for company!"

"You're *not* dying!"

Midnight was right. Curious wasn't dying. But an infection on a unicorn was a problem. A serious problem. It could mean only one thing that Midnight knew of.

"Festerlings!" she shouted.

"It's festering?" he asked.

"No, well, yes, it is. But no. I mean we're under attack."

"By what?"

"By a *fury* of *festerlings*!" she said.

And so now you know the other reason I told you about animal names. Because "fury" is the proper name for a group of festerling fairies.

And what are festerling fairies?

Well, just look, because here they come!

They came bursting out of the trees, a big black swarm—no, a *fury*—of them. They looked sort of like rotting ravens with cobwebs for wings. Or dead birds with the wings of flies in place of feathers. Long lizard tongues snaked out of their wicked beaks. Big, buglike eyes twitched on either side of their gray, rotten heads.

They were festerling fairies doing what festerling fairies did best.

Festering.

As they got closer, more spots appeared on Curious.

They popped into existence on his legs and back and chest. And even on the end of his nose.

"Ow, ow, ow," he said again.

And Wartle, because he didn't want to be left out, said, "Ow, ow, ow," as well.

But then Midnight felt it too.

The closer the fury of festerlings came, the worse the horses and Wartle all felt. And the worse they all looked.

Boils and blisters and pustules and pus and all kinds of ick was sprouting and bursting on their bodies. It was gross. Disgusting. Intolerable.

Midnight called on her fire and shot it out in a big blast.

Which, unfortunately, zoomed around the three not-quite-companions in a circle before swooping at Curious's head.

The unicorn ducked just in time, and a tree behind him exploded.

"Hey!" he shouted. "Watch where you blast that thing!"

"Sorry," said Midnight.

Then she coughed up some more fire.

This time her flame shot out in a long arc, high up into the air. But it went right past the festerlings, curved, and rained down—

—right where Curious had been until he jumped aside.

"Stop shooting me!" he said.

"I don't have much control," Midnight replied.

"Or any!" he said. Then he coughed, because the fes-terlings' corrupting magic was even getting inside him now.

Midnight was embarrassed. But she also realized her fire was just maybe seeking out the person she was the most upset with. Because even with the festerlings attacking, it was this dumb unicorn, who had ruined her first Plan and forced her to take him along, who was messing up her eve-ning. Still, she needed to control her fire, and that was her problem.

"Look," she said with a cough because now the fester-lings were getting inside her, too, "this is why I wanted a wispy wood wink."

And then she thought of another Plan.

"Give me the Absorbing Orb," she said.

"What? I'm not giving you the Orb."

"Give it to me now," she said. "I know how to save us."

And Curious stopped. Because maybe this had been her Plan all along. Maybe she just wanted to lure him into a trap. And get his Orb. And then leave him to cough and sputter while she ran away.

"Give it to me," she repeated.

"No," he said. "I don't trust you."

He felt bad saying it. But that was the truth. He couldn't trust her, could he? Not a night mare. Never trust a night mare. Wasn't that what they said?

They were Creatures of Wickedness.

And he was a unicorn, albeit one with a Scientific Mind.

What could he do?

What *should* he do?

He was going to have to do it quick, whatever it was.

What would you do?

9

SO WHAT DID CURIOUS DO?

Things weren't looking good for Curious.

Things weren't looking good for any of them, but Curious was by far the worst.

His legs were starting to give out. He was down on his knees—and remember he had four of them—and he was shaking and quaking from all the sputtering and coughing.

Unicorns never get sick. And they never feel very bad. So this was the worst he had ever felt in his young life.

And he had to do something about it. Because anything was better than this.

"W-W-Wartle," he cried.

"Wh-wh-what?" Wartle answered. He wasn't stuttering because he was sick. He was just generally up for whatever Curious wanted to do, and if the unicorn wanted to stutter, he would too.

"The Ab-Ab-Absorbing Orb," Curious said. "Gi-gi-give it to her!"

"Ri-ri-right," said Wartle promptly. But then he hesitated. Surely Curious didn't mean to give the Orb to the night mare? That didn't sound smart.

"C-C-Creature of W-W-Wickedness," Wartle pointed out.

"I kn-kn-know she's a C-C-Creature of W-W-Wickedness," Curious said, "but she's my—my—my only hope. Gi-gi-give her the Absorbing O-orb now!"

Well, that was clear enough.

"You're the b-b-boss!" said Wartle.

The puckle leapt from Curious's neck, sailing through the festerling-filled air, to land with a *thump* and an *oomph* on Midnight's back.

Midnight blew a surprised blast through her nostrils. It took all her willpower not to toss Wartle right off. She hated having anything on her back. All night mares do. Of course they do. And normally she wouldn't have put up with it. But she knew that this puckle was bringing her something she wanted—very, very much. She bit down her discomfort.

Even so, her hide shivered in that way horses do when they're trying to dislodge a bug. It made Wartle shiver too, and he giggled.

"The Absorbing Orb," she said. "Give it to me!"

Wartle held the Absorbing Orb in his hands. It glowed blue with the wispy wood wink inside. He looked around helplessly for some way to hand it to her. But, of course, that was problematic.

"No hands," he said. "You don't have any hands!"

"Give it to me anyway," said Midnight, who still didn't really appreciate the value of a good pair of hands.

Wartle's small beady eyes looked panicked. How could he give a horse something when she didn't have any hands to take it with?

Then he had an idea. Maybe not the best idea, but he was a puckle after all.

"Bye-bye, Winky!" he said.

He took the Absorbing Orb, and he crammed it in Midnight's ear. Deep in her ear.

"Owwwwwww!"

Oh, did she buck then!

She kicked her hind legs high in the air.

Wartle went sailing over her head, back through the festerling-filled air.

"Wheeeeeeeeeee!" he shouted as he flew.

Wartle landed with a *thump* and an *oomph* in a bush, a

black, prickly bush full of thorns and thistles, which is the only kind that grows in the Whisperwood.

"Ouch!" he cried. "Ow, ow, ow, ow, ow."

But the horses weren't listening.

Curious was too busy collapsing, as the fury of festerlings buzzed around his head. And Midnight was—

Midnight was too busy *feeling . . . strange.*

Like all her fires were being stoked, which they were. Like she had new energy. New focus.

And something about her felt *all lined up.*

Like metal shavings do when you hold a magnet near them. Or toy soldiers do when no one is looking.

But Midnight felt very organized and together and powerful.

And she *liked* it.

Midnight galloped up to the nearest festerling. She opened her mouth and she—

Hiccupped.

A loud, croaking, groaning hiiiiic-cup!

It wasn't what she had intended to do.

Not at all.

But it was enough.

A burst of red flame shot from her mouth.

But this time, the flame was concentrated. It was like a thin red beam.

It hit the first festerling, and it ricocheted.

Right into the second festerling. And it bounced off that one into a third.

A fourth.

A fifth.

The bolt of red night mare fire bounced all around the woods, striking every single festerling and lighting them up.

"Aaaaa-yaaaa-yoooo!" they all yelled at once. And "Ouch" and "Eeee" and "Ooooh." And then they turned and, flapping their burning, smoldering, crisping cob-webby feathers, they flew away as fast and as far as they could go.

They were gone. Leaving only a smell of burnt festerling behind them. It was an unpleasant smell, but a very welcome one considering.

"I did it!" shouted Wartle. "Me, me, me!" He was very pleased with himself and quite prepared to take all the credit, even if it wasn't his to take.

But Midnight didn't mind. She didn't notice.

She was staring down at her own muzzle, which was twisting into a new expression. One it hadn't had a lot of practice with.

It said, Midnight is very, very, *very* pleased with herself.

She was so excited, she threw back her head and she let out a loud, exultant *WHINNNNNYYY.*

Which is what a horse does when she is super excited.

And she almost did it again.

But she wasn't entirely selfish. She really could think about others when they needed thinking about. Maybe she ought to check on someone else before she whinnied again.

So she looked to the unicorn.

She needn't have bothered.

Curious's festering wounds were healing so fast they were shrinking away right before her eyes.

She saw that his horn was giving off a great golden glow. A *healing* glow.

By the time he climbed back to his feet, he was completely one hundred percent okeydokey.

Midnight pursed her lips. As the golden glow faded away, he was a perfectly perfect unicorn again.

By the moons, that was irritating!

But Curious looked at her with concern in his eyes.

That was irritating too.

"You're hurt," he said. He trotted toward her, and his horn began to glow again.

"Don't put that thing on me," she said.

"But you're still festering," he said. "You've got spots all over."

"Heal me, heal me!" cried Wartle. "I've got spots too."

Curious eyed the puckle. Apart from lying upside down in a thorn and thistle bush, he seemed okay. All his blisters and boils had faded away. Nothing really bothers puckles very much. Maybe because they're usually the ones doing the bothering.

"Are you actually hurt?" the unicorn asked.

"I bruised my bottom on the bush," said Wartle.

"I think that you will live," said Curious. He turned his attention back to Midnight.

"No way," she said. "I don't want any unicorn magic on me."

"Bottom!" said Wartle. "Bottom, bottom, bottom!"

"Please," Curious said. "It's not a big thing, really. I wouldn't count it as a favor I was doing you or anything."

Midnight eyed the glowing horn suspiciously. Her festerling wounds were nasty. They did feel rather gross and icky.

"Well, I suppose if it isn't a favor . . ."

"It's not."

"All right, then," she said. "As long as I never have to hear about it again."

"You won't."

She stood still, and Curious approached. His horn was shining its radiant light. Wherever he pointed it, her wounds cleared up and faded away. And she felt strength coming back to the healed patches. In fact, she felt quite good all over. Some places even felt better than before.

It really was quite amazing.

"How did you do that?" she asked. "Is it something you learn?"

"The horn magic," said Curious. "All unicorns can do it. Although for some reason, mares are better than stallions at it. The girls' magic is just stronger than the boys'. Say, your magic is pretty strong."

"My fire is always strong," said Midnight.

"But it was very tightly focused," observed Curious. "Is that why you wanted to eat a wispy wood wink? To focus your fire?"

"If you must know, yes."

"Did you know a wispy wood wink could do that? Have you eaten one before?"

"No, I haven't eaten one before. I just thought a different color fire might change my fire a little."

"So you were conducting an Experiment!"

"What? No I wasn't."

"Yes, you were," insisted Curious. "You were conducting a proper scientific Experiment. It's just like what I do."

"It's nothing like what you do," said Midnight. Being compared to a unicorn really irritated her. She broke away from him, moving into a canter.

"We've wasted enough time," she said. "I've got places to be. I've got to reach the Curse before midnight."

"Why before midnight?" asked Curious.

"Because I do," she insisted.

Curious didn't like it at all.

This is it, he thought. *The first trap was so she could get her hooves on my Absorbing Orb, and now she's bringing me to the Curse.*

But she had saved him. At least twice now. Why would she do that if she was just going to take him to the Curse for another trap? His Scientific Mind didn't think that made sense. And Curious started to get curious.

So he followed her.

"Can't you find the Curse later?"

"No, it has to be tonight."

"Why tonight?"

Midnight sighed. "Because tonight the moons line up."

Curious glanced at the sky. "So?"

"So when the moons line up, we have the Stomp."

Curious had never heard of the Stomp. Of course, not knowing about a thing made him very curious. Which is to say, very much himself. So now he was really curious.

"What's the Stomp?" he asked.

"Only the most important night of the month," said Midnight.

"If it's so important, why haven't I heard of it?"

"It's for night mares only."

"Okay, but what do you do at a Stomp?"

"We don't stomp unicorns if that's what you're worried about."

"No, really? What is it?"

"It's a Stomp. You stomp! Why do you think it's called a Stomp?"

"But why do you stomp at a Stomp?"

"Look, we have these rocks called the Silent Stones. A long time ago, I think they kept all the fairies out of the Glistening Isles. Only they don't really work anymore. Their magic has all drained away. But at the Stomp, we can give them a little bit of magic. Just enough to keep us safe by the stones at night. But only at midnight and only once a month when the moons are right. And it gets us through a month until the next Stomp."

"Could I watch it?" Curious asked.

"Absolutely not."

"But I'm really . . ."

"Curious?"

Curious nodded.

"Well, too bad. Look, if you were there, the Curse would go crazy. Then it really would be a Unicorn Stomp. Not a Stomp Stomp."

Curious grumbled, but he knew she was telling the truth. And he didn't want to be the main attraction at a

Unicorn Stomp. He was wondering what could be done about it, when Midnight slowed down to a trot.

"Shhh," she said. "We're getting close."

"But you said I couldn't go."

"Not to where I'm going," she explained. "To where you're going."

Then she trotted off the path, and Curious saw a little clearing in the woods. There was a small, rocky hill, and in the hill, the mouth of a cave.

"What is this place?" he asked.

"It's a cave," she said.

"But why are we here?"

"You can wait here until morning," she said.

Curious looked at the dark opening.

"In there?" he said.

"It's just a cave."

"Yes," said Curious. "Dark caves aren't really a thing on my side of the river. The only caves we have are crystal caves, and they're never very dark."

Midnight snorted.

"It's perfectly safe. Or at least it's pretty safe. I'm fairly sure it's safe. Safe-ish."

"I don't know about this," said Curious.

"Look," said Midnight, "I have to be at the Silent Stones for the Stomp, and I don't have any more time. You can't come. So you can either wait here for me where you're safe, you can wander about where something nasty might spot you, or you can try finding your own way back to your Blessing on your own."

Curious shook his mane in frustration. But he didn't see that he had any options. So he trotted into the cave.

It was dark inside, of course, but fairly dry. It went back farther than he could see. He turned around and faced outward.

"You'll return in the morning?" he said.

"Yes," said Midnight.

"You promise?"

Midnight sighed.

"I promise. Now I have to go."

"What if someone else comes in?" he asked.

"They won't," said Midnight.

"How can you be sure?" asked Curious.

"Because they're all afraid of the Slumbering Cindersloth."

"Slumbering Cinder-what!?!" yelled Wartle.

Curious was so startled by the puckle's outburst that he leapt off all four hooves at once.

"Relax," said Midnight. "The Slumbering Cindersloth almost never wakes up anymore. That's why they call her 'slumbering,' right? So I'm sure she won't wake up tonight.

Probably not anyway. Maybe keep quiet just to be safe. Safe-ish."

And then she turned and cantered away, leaving Curious very curious, and more than a little nervous, about being alone with whatever a Slumbering Cindersloth was.

But Curious could never worry for long. Not when he was so curious. And he was so curious he itched.

"I want to see the Stomp," he said. "I really, really, really want to see the Stomp."

"You don't even know what a Stomp is," Wartle pointed out.

"That's why I want to see it," said Curious. "Do you think if I'm really, really sneaky we can spy on the Stomp? And we can slip back to this cave right afterward. Midnight won't even know we were gone."

"I don't know," said Wartle.

"As long as the Curse doesn't see us, it'll be fine."

"As long as nothing else does either," said Wartle.

Curious thought about that.

"But they won't," he said. "Because the *Stomp* keeps Wicked Fairies away. So it will work! What could go wrong?"

"Lots of things," said Wartle. And though he wasn't right about much, he was right about this.

10

A NIGHT MARE TO REMEMBER

Midnight was glad to be free of the unicorn. Even if it was only temporarily. Oh, she was tempted to just leave him where he was. That was a really attractive notion to be sure.

But she'd have to go back for him eventually.

And the Slumbering Cindersloth? It *probably* wouldn't wake up before she returned, right? Probably not. But either way, Curious would have to leave the cave eventually. He couldn't stay there forever. And it would sort of—kind of—maybe be her fault if something else ate him when he did. After all, she had dragged him deeper into the Whisperwood than he would have gone by himself. Of course, he never should have jumped in the river in the first place.

Stupid, stupid unicorn.

But unicorns *were* stupid. So maybe he couldn't help himself. It was just one more reason that she was glad she was a night mare and not one of *them*. Or she would be glad, if *they* didn't make her live in the Whisperwood. They thought they were *so good*. But night mares were better than unicorns, right? No unicorn had ever jumped in the river to save a night mare. So she was better than he was. And if something ate him before he told any of his snooty friends, well, no one would ever know.

She glanced at the sky. The smaller moon was moving into position right in front of the larger one. Together, they looked like a giant eye in the sky—a big silvery orb with a large black pupil rolling across its surface toward the center. This meant that it was almost time for the Stomp. The Stomp was only ever held on nights like this.

She had an odd thought, which was that Curious would enjoy watching the Stomp. Too bad he couldn't see it, then. Too bad? The Stomp wasn't for outsiders. Even *scientific* ones. It had nothing to do with science. The Stomp was about fire, and excitement, and old, old magic, and, well, *stomping,* of course.

Midnight couldn't wait. She hadn't been in a Stomp since she was one year old. Her first and only time. That one had ended badly with a big *boom-bada-boom.* Which wasn't *really* her fault. Because she didn't know then how wild her fire could be. But it was more her fault than anyone else's. Because it was *her* fire. So the herd had told her very firmly, No More Stomping For You, Midnight. And ever since, she had been Midnight of the Uncontrollable Fire. Midnight Who Was Always Causing Explosions. Midnight, Trouble for the Curse, and Oh, Midnight, Why Can't You Just Be Like Everybody Else?

But tonight would be different. Because tonight she had a wispy wood wink trapped in an Absorbing Orb crammed in her ear. So she must be different. And she was sure the difference was a good difference.

She thought about how impressed all the night mares were going to be when they saw her stomping. It was going to be grand and glorious and very, very fun. She was going to be the best stomper in the whole entire history of the Stomp.

So she practically raced as she followed the path through the Whisperwood that led to the Curse's Hidden Glen. She heard the neighing and snorting of horses up ahead and her heart did a little *bump-thumpa-bump.* She felt very excited and very energetic.

For all of about two minutes.

"WHERE HAVE YOU BEEN?" roared a voice.

Midnight knew the voice. It was often roaring at her. It always sounded angry or disappointed or maybe just plain tired when it did so. So she wasn't surprised when she saw a horse standing before her.

It was, of course, Sabledusk doing the roaring.

Who's Sabledusk?

Only the biggest, strongest, fiercest night mare in the entire herd. You had to be tough if you wanted to lead the Curse, because let's face it, horses with burning hooves and fire snorting out their nostrils can't be led by just anyone. I couldn't do it. Could you?

But Sabledusk could. And she did.

She was the head night mare. She was large and in charge. She was something else, too, very specific to Midnight. But we'll get to that in a moment. Because right now Sabledusk is tapping her hoof impatiently and waiting for an answer. And it's an answer that Midnight really doesn't want to give.

"Um, well," said Midnight. "I've just been out. For a little stroll. That's it, a stroll. To, um, the cave of the Slumbering Cindersloth."

"The Cindersloth," said Sabledusk. "For all this time?" She didn't sound like she believed Midnight. The cave wasn't very far away and, honestly, wasn't very interesting.

"Uh, yes, the Cindersloth," said Midnight, stammering in a way that said she didn't really believe herself either. "And maybe the River Restless."

"The *river*?" said Sabledusk. "You should never go out at night when there are Fairy Creatures about! And you should positively absolutely never go as far as the River Restless."

"I know. I got restless too," said Midnight, her voice going very small. All this time, Midnight had been looking at the ground and shuffling her hooves. But now she risked a glance upward. When Sabledusk got really mad, her mane burst into yellow flame. It was really impressive and scary and pretty all at the same time. But it was generally a bad sign if you were the reason her mane was burning yellow. It wasn't burning now, which meant that she was only sort of mad. Not maximum mad. Not super-duper mad. That was good.

Midnight brightened.

"But I came back! Just in time for the Stomp. I have a feeling it's going to be a good one!" She tossed her head to indicate the moons, which had just about lined up.

Sabledusk looked up as well. She saw the moons were doing their thing. She didn't really have time to sort out Midnight.

Sabledusk sighed a big, long sigh of air that made her lips all wobbly.

"Get inside," she said with a voice full of resignation. "We'll talk about this later."

Midnight shook her head in a horsey way of saying "okay, okay" and then she trotted forward.

Now, I'm sure you've never seen the secret home of the Curse of night mares deep within the Whisperwood. No human ever has. It was a big, broad, and mostly circular glen that was open to the sky. Inside the glen there were two rings of twenty-two old stones arranged in two circles, one of twelve stones and one of ten stones, and there was a twenty-third stone in the center. A couple of them had fallen over, and a couple of them had lost their tops. Nearly all of them were cracked and chipped, but they were still very impressive.

All the still standing stones were very tall. They were carved with strange runes that no one could read (though night mares don't read anyway). Moss grew all over them and here or there a vine. And they seemed somehow maybe just a little bit, well, don't think me crazy, but they seemed just a little bit *alive*. Like they were sleeping, maybe. Or waiting for something, perhaps.

These were, of course, the Silent Stones. Once upon a time, they were magical, but their magic was mostly gone now. But even so, fairies and Fairy Creatures avoided them if they could. That was usually good, but tonight it was unfortunate for Midnight. Because Midnight had forgotten that wispy wood winks were Fairy Creatures. So when she trotted forward she got a reminder.

Just as Midnight stepped between the two stones, the wispy wood wink twitched and jerked. It was trapped in an Absorbing Orb and Wartle had crammed the orb as tight in her ear as he could fit it. So the wink didn't get loose and neither did the orb. But Midnight's head was pulled back and her neck twisted.

Sabledusk snorted in surprise.

"Stop fooling around and get in here," she said.

"I'm not fooling around," said Midnight. She blew an angry blast and stepped forward again.

The wispy wood wink thrashed around inside her ear again. This time it forced her head down, between her knees, so that she almost folded over.

"What's the matter with you?" asked Sabledusk. "You're not under a spell, are you?" She looked over Midnight's head, into the darkness of the Whisperwood, in case any Wicked Fairies were about and casting evil magics. She didn't see any, but you never knew with Wicked Fairies and evil magics.

"No, no," said Midnight, who was worried Sabledusk might spot the crystal orb in her ear. "I'm fine. It's just a horsefly. Trying to bite me on the bum."

"I don't see any horseflies," said Sabledusk suspiciously.

"There it is, there," said Midnight, as convincingly as she could. "There it goes." And then, under her breath, she said, "Bzzzz, bzzz, bzzzz."

"All riiiiiight," said Sabledusk. "Just get in here where it's safe."

"I'm trying," said Midnight. And with that she shook her head savagely, rattling the wink in her ear. It must have gotten dizzy, because it settled down to being only slightly twitchy. Then she strode forward into the stone circle.

"You're here!" cried her friend Vision. "I thought I'd never see you again. Not after you jumped in the river."

"Nonsense," said Midnight, trotting over to Vision. "Don't I always come back from a Plan?"

"Yes," said Vision. "That's true. But I thought maybe this Plan was different. This time you were on the other side of the river. And that's never been in one of your Plans before."

"Hush," said Midnight quickly.

"With a unicorn," said Vision.

"Shush," said Midnight quickly.

"That you *saved*," said Vision.

"Hush and shush and shut it too," said Midnight. "Look, I'll tell you all about it after the Stomp, but you have to keep quiet. I don't want Sabledusk or anyone else to find out what I've been up to."

"That's because you know what they will say."

"Yes," said Midnight. "They will say that unicorns are evil, and I should have let him drown."

"And they'll say that because it's *true*."

Midnight thought about that. The unicorn was annoying, but she wasn't sure she'd call him evil.

"Curious isn't *evil*," she said. "He's stupid. And he thinks I'm a Creature of Wickedness, but that's only because it's what he's been taught."

"You've been talking with him!"

"I rescued him. Of course I talked to him!"

"Midnight, this is really too much."

"You won't tell on me, will you?"

Vision tilted her head and gave Midnight an "I don't know about this" look.

"Please," said Midnight. It wasn't a word she used often, and Vision knew it.

"All right," she said. "But you have to promise me you won't go running off with any more unicorns."

"I promise." Midnight thought that she wasn't exactly lying. After all, she wasn't going to go running off with any *more* unicorns. She was just going to go running off in the morning with the unicorn she *already had*.

She had just about breathed a sigh of relief, when someone barked behind them—

"Unicorns? What unicorns?"

They had been overheard. And by the worst horse imaginable.

Old Sooty. The oldest of the night mares. She was so old her hair wasn't black. Her hide was more of a dirty gray with spots. She didn't have fire anymore. Just puffs of sooty smoke that appeared when she coughed. Which is why she was called Old Sooty.

Now, it's important to remember that Midnight had once set Old Sooty's tail on fire. That had been an accident. Mostly. Probably. Which is why Old Sooty hated Midnight and why she was always trying to get her kicked out of the herd.

"Unicorns?" said Midnight, and she blinked her eyes so innocently. "Who was talking about unicorns?"

"You were," said Old Sooty.

"Me? No," said Midnight. "I was talking about queasy thorns."

" 'Queasy thorns'?" said Old Sooty skeptically.

"Yes, you know, those nasty thorns that make you feel all sick when they stick you. Vision saw some over there"— she gestured to the woods on her left—"and she was just warning me about them. Because she's a good friend." And now Midnight was speaking very slowly and deliberately. "And she wouldn't. Want. To. Ever. See. Me. Get. Into. Any. Trouble."

"Vision, is that true?" said Old Sooty.

Vision's eyes darted between Midnight and Old Sooty.

"That's right," said Vision with a sigh. "We were talking about queasy thorns." She gritted her teeth and spoke slowly and deliberately. "And I don't. Want. To. See. Midnight. Get. Into. Any. More. Trouble."

Snort, snorted Old Sooty. But this made her go *cough, cough* and puff black smoke.

"Midnight is—*COUGH, COUGH*—always trouble," she said. "That should be—*PUFF, PUFF*—her name."

Old Sooty trotted away in a cloud of smoke. Being fireless, she couldn't partake in the Stomp, so she went to the edge of the outermost stone circle to get a good view.

"Thank you," said Midnight.

"Old Sooty has taken the best spot," said Vision. "But you can still stand over there." She pointed to a spot on the opposite side of the glen. "It's not too bad a view."

"Oh, no," said Midnight. "I won't be watching tonight."

"What do you mean you won't be watching?" said Vision, starting to get worried again. "How can you not watch the Stomp?"

"Oh, I'll watch," said Midnight. "I just mean watching isn't all I'm going to be doing."

Vision's eyes started to widen.

"Midnight, you know you're not allowed—"

"Don't worry, friend Vision," said Midnight, drawing herself up tall. "For my Plan has gone according to plan. I predict this is going to be the best Stomp ever. This is going to be a night to remember."

"But I *am* worried," said Vision. "Your Plans don't ever go as you expect."

And, of course, Vision was right. But Midnight was right too. Because the Stomp was about to go horribly wrong. But it was certainly going to be a night to remember.

Are you curious? Well, so is a certain unicorn. And he's hiding with a nervous puckle at the edge of the woods. And he's eager to see what happens next. Don't keep him waiting! Read on!

✿ 11 ✿

THE SILENT STONES . . . OR ARE THEY?

This was it. This was the Stomp. All the nightmares—except of course for Old Sooty—had taken up positions between the stones of the outer ring. Sabledusk stood by herself before the central stone looking very imposing and leaderlike. But Midnight wasn't with them yet. The Curse didn't know she was planning on stomping. Sabledusk would have said no if Midnight had asked. Midnight planned to join in only once the Stomp started.

Yes, thought Midnight, *this is definitely a Plan where it is better to ask forgiveness later than permission first.*

As the moons moved into position, horses neighed and nickered. They shifted their hooves in nervous anticipation.

"Quiet!" yelled Sabledusk.

Everyone got very quiet and still.

Sabledusk turned her fiery red eyes to the moons.

"Let the Stomp begin," she cried.

Then Sabledusk reared up on her back legs and let out a loud and glorious whinny.

When she came down, her hooves struck the ground in front of the big center stone with a loud smack.

Fire burst from her hooves, shooting to each of the horses in the circle. *Whoosh! Whoosh! Whoosh!*

They all rose up into the air and whinnied too.

And when each night mare came back down, their own hooves struck fire too.

Every night mare's fire was a different color, from blazing red to vibrant orange to brilliant yellow. And then all the night mares began to stomp at once.

Stomp stompa stomp stompa stomp stomp stomp!

The fires raced along the ground and arced through the air.

Magic Motes appeared. Glowing golden lights, conjured out of thin air by the Stomp.

Not wispy wood winks, who were all about trying to lure you into the river. These were sparks of loose magic. They whirled around the night mares and fed the Silent Stones.

The once-faint runes carved into their surfaces glimmered in the night with reddish-goldish light.

There was a humming, like someone singing far away, or maybe right behind your ear but very softly.

The Silent Stones were singing again.

Midnight was so excited.

Because now was her chance.

She leapt, all four legs off the ground.

She landed in the space right between the inner and the outer rings.

The night mares were so surprised to see her that they all stopped stomping.

The Magic Motes started to fade.

The Silent Stones started to go silent again.

Sabledusk started to yell.

This would have all been very bad, but honestly, pretty much what was expected of Midnight.

But Midnight had an Absorbing Orb crammed in her ear. So she wasn't afraid.

She picked one hoof *up.*

She brought it *down.*

And her wild fire wasn't *wild* at all.

It shot from her hoof in a perfectly straight line, a great gleaming bolt of deep-red energy that raced right to the center stone.

Now the center stone glowed brighter than it had ever

glowed before, its magical energy radiating to all the other stones.

The night mares were astonished.

Their mouths dropped open. Their ears twitched up and their tails lifted into the air.

They said, "Is that Midnight?" "Look at her go." "I wish my fire were that strong."

Midnight stomped, stomped, stomped.

And the night mares cheered and stomped with her.

The Magic Motes twirled around Midnight. They seemed to like her best.

"Oh, Midnight," said Sabledusk. For the first time she didn't sound disappointed when she said it. "You can finally control your fire. I'm so, so proud of you."

And Midnight, hearing that, was happy.

So began a wild and woolly dance, with Midnight as the leader. She would weave a great and beautiful pattern of light. It looked like constellations drawn upon the ground. And the Silent Stones sang.

It was the best and brightest moment of Midnight's entire life.

Everyone saw how amazing her fire was when it wasn't *wild*.

And all the night mares were glad.

Because, you see, the Stomp wasn't just for fun and

pretty. The Stomp had an important purpose. It recharged the Silent Stones. Not with all the power they used to have in the days before the fairies came to the Glistening Isles. But with just enough power to drive the Wicked Fairies and Wicked Fairy Creatures out of the glen for another month.

It was the Stomp that kept the Curse safe through the dangerous nights of the Whisperwood. They could sleep at night without Wicked Fairies and Wicked Fairy Creatures tiptoeing in to hex and hassle them while they slept. So now you know why Midnight was never allowed to Stomp when her fire was wild and explode-y.

But tonight she was the *hero,* the one who would charge the Silent Stones up higher than they'd ever been before.

And it was all due to the wispy wood wink trapped in an Absorbing Orb and crammed in her ear.

Uh-oh. There was a flaw in Midnight's great Plan.

A pretty big flaw.

Have you spotted it?

The flaw is this:

The Silent Stones, when they are working correctly, drive the Wicked Fairies and Fairy Creatures away.

A wispy wood wink is a Wicked Fairy.

See the problem now?

As the Stones grew in power, the wispy wood wink in Midnight's ear became more uncomfortable.

At first, Midnight was too busy stomping and dancing and leaping about to notice. But inside her ear the wispy wood wink was twitching, jerking, thrashing. . . .

That little wispy wood wink twisted so hard that it dislodged the Absorbing Orb. It flew right out of Midnight's ear—

—sailing across the glen, a blue glowing projectile streaking through the sky.

Every night mare wondered what a wispy wood wink in an Absorbing Orb was doing in their Hidden Glen.

But they didn't wonder long, because Midnight's fire—which was all riled up from stomping—had lost its *focus.*

And now it was wild and explode-y again.

Ragged, jagged bolts of blazing energy curved and twisted, zigged and zagged. Where it struck the stones, explosions went off.

The Magic Motes twirled in the air like a swarm of angry bees.

The glowing runes carved in the Silent Stones flared hot once and then went dead. The Stones fell silent.

Then, with a great, loud *bang,* the center stone fell over.

The night was very quiet. All the night mares were quiet too.

Except for Sabledusk, who looked at Midnight and said, "Oh, Midnight. What have you done?"

Poor Midnight went from her dream come true to her worst nightmare.

"I—I—I—" she said.

But before she could think of what to say, Old Sooty leapt into the Whisperwood.

"Spy!" she roared. "Spy! Spy! Spy! I've caught a spy!"

Old Sooty drove a horse from the shelter of the trees into the moonslight.

There in front of her, looking very embarrassed, was a unicorn with a Scientific Mind.

Midnight knew that her worst nightmare had gotten even worse and was now her double worst nightmare.

The Curse had captured Curious.

❧ 12 ❧

LET'S PLAY STOMP THE UNICORN

"I—I—I can explain," said Midnight. Although she probably couldn't. In fact, she had no idea what sort of an expla-
nation was going to get her out of this mess. She had led a
unicorn right to the Curse's Hidden Glen on the night of the
Stomp, and knocked over the center stone. As messes went,
this was the worst mess ever.

Curious had been shoved next to the big center stone
where it had fallen over. He still had that silly U-shaped
bit of metal ringed around his horn. The night mares surrounded him on all sides. They were stamping their burning

hooves. They were looking at him with very angry looks. They were stamping their hooves and looking at Midnight that way too.

But it was Sabledusk's look that hurt the most.

The leader of the Curse kept shaking her mane and twitching her ears as if she just couldn't believe it.

She looked at Midnight with a deep, sad disappointment. The worst kind of disappointment, just after you had begun to hope that maybe someone wasn't the complete mess you thought they were, only it turned out that you were wrong. They were an even worse mess than you knew.

"Daughter," she said sorrowfully, "what have you done?"

Midnight couldn't answer. She was just realizing that the herd wasn't protected from the Fairy Creatures at night. And nights in the Whisperwood were bad. She had really, really done it this time.

But wait. Did Sabledusk just call Midnight "daughter"? Why, yes she did.

And that is because Midnight was Sabledusk's daughter.

You'll remember that I said that night mares just started popping up after the Fairy Queen invited the unicorns to live on the Glistening Isles. No one knew how the night mares got there. No one brought them. But they appeared. *Pop, pop, pop.* And not even the night mares themselves knew where they came from.

But a night mare would just appear, usually fully grown,

but sometimes young like Midnight. They were always on fire. All snorty and blazing. But they were confused. Disoriented. They didn't know who they were or how they got to the Glistening Isles.

Oh, they had vague memories. Scary ones. Fuzzy memories of riding hard through human dreams. But nothing before that. Or maybe something so bad they mostly forgot what it was. But if they were on the north side of the island, the unicorns would drive them south, and they would find the Curse. And if they were on the south side of the island, then they'd find the Curse anyway. Or the Curse would find them.

Sabledusk found Midnight, burning hot in the woods at night in a big ring of fire surrounded by scorched trees. Midnight had been wild and angry, but she had also seemed sad and lost.

Something between them had felt so strong that Sabledusk had proclaimed Midnight her daughter. She had named her Midnight, because that is when she had appeared.

So now you know why Midnight hadn't been kicked out of the Curse already for all the trouble she caused. But this trouble that was happening right now was the worst trouble ever in Midnight's young life. Maybe even the mighty Sabledusk couldn't save her this time.

"Midnight," said Sabledusk. "What is the unicorn doing here?"

Midnight looked to Curious. The night mares were poking at him with burning hooves. He was trying very hard not to panic and absolutely not enjoying himself.

"Ah, well," said Midnight, wondering what she could say that could make things better.

"He's a spy!" coughed Old Sooty. "She's in cahoots with him."

"Nonsense," said Midnight. "I've never gotten in a cahoot in my life! Anyway, Curious isn't a spy."

"You know his *name*?" said Sabledusk. And now maybe there were a few little yellow sparks starting to burn in her mane.

"If I could say a few words," said Curious, straining his neck to see over the horses around him.

Sabledusk turned to the unicorn, and although they were very angry, his tormentors stepped back to give her a view.

"Thank you," said Curious, trotting forward. "Greetings, oh Creature of Wickedness," he called out. And that was absolutely the wrong thing to say. Flames were bursting from manes all around now. "There is no need to fear me. I do not come here intending harm. I have been led by the quest for scientific knowledge."

"No one here fears you," said Sabledusk. "But how does my daughter know your name?"

Behind her back, Midnight was shaking her head vigorously *no, no, no.* Unfortunately, Curious didn't take the hint.

"Well, she saved my life," he said. "It was only polite to tell her my name after that."

"She saved you?"

"She saved him," said Vision. She glanced at Midnight apologetically. "That unicorn was being drowned by some kelpies. Midnight dove into the river and rescued him."

"You *dove* into the river?" said Sabledusk. "You *rescued* him? Why would you do that?"

"Because they wouldn't do it for us," said Midnight.

"Well, of course they wouldn't," said Sabledusk. "No unicorn would lift a hoof to help a night mare. So why would you do it for them?"

Midnight lifted her eyes to her mother.

"To prove we're better than they are," she said. "To show we aren't the Creatures of Wickedness they think we are."

"But what does that matter?" said Sabledusk. "Who cares what *they* think? Unicorns and night mares can never get along. A unicorn will never see itself as anything other than good and right and true, and they will always see us as their opposites."

"I'm no one's opposite," said Midnight.

"Perhaps not, Daughter. But to prove that, you have brought a unicorn here. And you have destroyed the power of the Silent Stones. You have hurt us worse than any unicorn."

"Stomp her!" shouted Old Sooty. "Stomp her and the unicorn!"

"Yes," several other night mares cried. "Stomp them. Stomp them both."

Sabledusk looked worried. Although she was the leader of the herd, she would have a hard time saving her daughter if the whole of the Curse was against it.

"Please," said Midnight. "I didn't mean any harm. And neither did Curious. He's an idiot, but he didn't mean any harm."

"Hey," said Curious. "I'm not an idiot. I have a Scientific Mind."

"A what?" said Sabledusk.

"I'm a scientist," said Curious. "I'm fascinated by your stones here. They were glowing green a moment ago. And their runes were reddish gold. There were motes of golden lights around them. And your fires—they burned from yellow to orange to red. Perhaps if I could understand them . . ."

"It's magic," said Sabledusk. "What's to understand?"

She turned to the Curse.

"No one is to stomp my daughter," she said. And when there were mutterings and grumblings, fire flared from Sabledusk's mane and she said, *"NO ONE!"*

"But," Sabledusk added, "that does not mean she won't be punished. I hereby proclaim that Midnight is banished."

Banished.

Alone in the Whisperwood.

Forever.

This was worse than being stomped.

"No," said Midnight. "No!"

"I am sorry, child, but you leave me no choice. And as for the unicorn, the unicorn we will stomp."

"Wait? What?" said Curious.

"Oh, now, wait a moment," said Midnight. "This really isn't necessary. I promise you."

"It's very necessary," said Sabledusk. "He has seen the Hidden Glen. He's seen the Stomp. And anyway, the Curse is angry and they want to stomp someone. So better a unicorn than my daughter."

The night mares all came forward in an angry rush.

Curious fell back. He retreated until he was against the fallen center stone. Then he had nowhere else to go.

Things didn't look good.

"Wait!" cried Midnight, and she leapt in front of Curious.

Sabledusk stared at her daughter.

"You put yourself in our way?"

"No! I mean maybe. I mean yes."

Sabledusk's mane blazed in yellow fire.

"Very well," she roared. "Then you and he can—"

But we won't get to know what she would have said next, because just then someone new entered the glen. Someone who didn't belong there either. Someone who, I'm sorry to say, always spoke in rhymes. . . .

"Oh, what a mess, I do confess
I never thought to see
A horse with horn look so forlorn
'midst fiery black ponies."

Jack o' the Hunt was inside the Silent Stones, where no Wicked Fairy had ever stood before.

But he wasn't standing. Oh, no, he was riding.

On a new night mare that had never been seen before.

And although there was only one Jack, and there were a great many fierce and fiery horses, all the night mares backed away and snorted nervously when he approached.

Yes, all those fearsome night mares were afraid of Jack. There was just something about the pumpkin-headed fairy that spooked them right down deep in the core of their being.

From the bottoms of their hooves to the tops of their heads.

Maybe *especially* the tops of their heads.

Sabledusk was the first to master her fear. She was leader of the Curse, after all.

"What is your business here, Jack?" she said.

The big pumpkin head smiled and the eyes stretched wide in the shell. He gestured around the glen.

"Your stones I see have lost their power.
They've wilted like a dying flower.
And as the rocks have lost their shine,
I come tonight to take what's mine!"

Midnight and Curious looked at one another. Was Jack after Midnight? Or Curious?

Or was he after something else?

Jack o' the Hunt came closer and closer.

And closer still.

IS THIS THE END? BUT THERE ARE STILL SO MANY CHAPTERS LEFT.

The poor new night mare carrying Jack o' the Hunt looked absolutely *terrified.*

She tried to buck and toss him off. But a ropey pumpkin vine twined through her mouth like a bit and bridle. Jack gave it a savage tug, and the night mare had to ride where he commanded.

As he rode, the candle shining in his head cast beams of light that swept back and forth across the glen.

Jack's lights were so mesmerizing that it was hard to look anywhere but at the big orange gourd. He was hypnotic. He had everyone's attention.

Almost.

Curious, even afraid, was still curious.

Curious couldn't help but look everywhere.

At Jack, sure. But also at the ground. At the stones. Even at the new night mare.

Curious saw that she was young, maybe just about his age or a little older. And her flaming red eyes were wide open in fear.

You'd be afraid too if Pumpkin Jack rode on your back.

So even though she was a Creature of Wickedness, Curious felt sorry for her. Because even though his Scientific Mind often got in the way, Curious also had a heart.

Then he noticed something more.

The new night mare had a weird marking on her forehead. It was pale and star-shaped. It reminded him of something. Or someone.

Curious noticed two other things.

Remember how the wispy wood wink had twitched itself right out of Midnight's ear? Well, it hadn't gotten very far. Still in the Absorbing Orb, it lay in a patch of grass right beside one of the stones. Its blue glow was mostly hidden in the tall grass.

And the other thing Curious noticed?

Wartle, of course!

Had you forgotten about him? Most folks do. But Curious hadn't forgotten him. And Wartle hadn't forgotten Curious. Poor little Wartle was a Fairy Creature too. He didn't like the singing of the Silent Stones any more than the wispy wood wink had. So when the stones were singing, Wartle had ducked through a tiny fairy door set in a rather large mushroom and escaped into Elsewhither. But he didn't want to desert his friend Curious. So he had opened the door just a crack, peeking through from the other side to see what he could do to help. Which, sadly, wasn't much.

Jack o' the Hunt looked down at Midnight and Curious from atop this terrified new night mare.

"Although I thought you rather weak,
You found your way across the creek.
But now of fear you both do reek,
So you shall give me what I seek!"

With a squelchy, vegetable-y sound, pumpkin vines sprouted up from the ground. Their leaves curled like long green fingers, and they reached for Midnight and Curious.

"Wait," said the ever-curious Curious. "What do you mean what you seek? What are you looking for?"

Jack waved his fingers in their tattered gloves. His nasty vines leapt forward, striking out like snakes.

But before Midnight and Curious could be trapped, Sabledusk threw herself into the path of the oncoming plants.

Did you think she wouldn't? Oh, Sabledusk might be disappointed in Midnight, but throwing yourself in the way of nasty pumpkin vines was just something you did for your daughter, if you had one.

The vines struck Sabledusk and not Midnight and not Curious. Jack roared in frustration, and he made complicated flappy motions with his hands. But the vines were already roping around and around Sabledusk, who was fast disappearing in a growing mass of leafy green.

"Mother!" shouted Midnight.

From out of this green lump, Sabledusk's fiery eye found Midnight.

"Run!" she shouted. Then her eye was covered in the coiling pumpkin tendrils and she disappeared from view.

Midnight was horrified.

But Curious shoved his shoulder into hers.

"Run means run," he said. "Now, it means! Run, run!"

Midnight ran.

And Curious with her.

And Wartle realized he'd have to do something if he didn't want to be left behind. He darted from his little fairy door, and he scampered across the glen.

"Winky," he cried as he ran.

The puckle scooped up the Absorbing Orb, and then, with a great jump, he leapt onto Curious's back.

Away they charged, racing through the Whisperwood. Which was no safe place to be at night but safer than staying with a pumpkin named Jack.

Midnight jumped fallen logs and Curious ducked low limbs. And Wartle clung to Curious's mane and yelled "Yippeeeee!" and "Walla, walla, whoa!" Branches tore at their flanks. Rocks tripped up their hooves. Strange voices cried from the shadows.

Dark things crept among the trees. They flapped overhead. They slithered underfoot. And any other night, they would have been deadly dangerous to our two horses.

But tonight Midnight and Curious didn't have time to stop and be threatened. Because Jack o' the Hunt was hunting them.

And when the dark things saw who was after the two horses, they crept aside and flapped away and slithered off. Because not one of them was brave enough to get in Pumpkin Jack's way.

Jack on the hunt was a terrible thing.

The red light of the new night mare glowed through the trees, blending with the beams of Jack's candle. The hollow horrid laughing of a pumpkin shell that shouldn't be able to laugh at all echoed through the night.

"Where are we going?" Curious asked.

"Where we were always going," replied Midnight.

Before Curious could complain about this answer, pumpkin vines made a grab for him, and he had to jump and twist and duck.

Jack o' the Hunt never seemed to tire. That evil Wicked Fairy didn't care how the night mare felt at all. He would ride her until she dropped or burned up in flame.

But then Midnight and Curious broke from the Whisperwood into the open. They were coming again to a bank of the River Restless. That was no good. Because they still couldn't cross the river, not with kelpies swimming in it, angry at them already. They would be trapped between woods and water with nowhere to go.

Nowhere!

⚛ 14 ⚛

WHY IS HE MAD?

Jack was almost upon them.

Then Curious saw a big flat wooden thing moored to the bank of the river. And just as he saw it, Midnight yelled out, "Wake up! Wake up! Poor Mad Tom, we have need of you. Awake and shove off!"

A figure arose from where it had been sleeping on the wooden thing. It peered at the night mare and the unicorn and the laughing, snarling pumpkin that chased them.

Quick as a flash the figure began to busy itself. Curious

saw that the wooden thing was a big flat raft, and the figure was something he'd never expected to see in the Glistening Isles. Not unicorn, not night mare, not fairy.

The figure was a human being!

Curious had never seen a human before. He had only heard stories about them, passed down from unicorn to unicorn.

Midnight reached the edge of the river and leapt into the air. Her hooves traced arcs of flame in the sky. She landed with a *thud* upon the raft.

And Curious followed after her. With a blue arc from the light of a wispy wood wink and a *thud* of his own and a "Wheeeee!" from Wartle.

Poor Mad Tom teetered and tottered as the force of two horses set the raft to bobbing on the waters. But taking a long pole, he shoved off, and the raft began to slide from the shore and into the current.

Jack o' the Hunt reared his night mare to a halt at the edge of the River Restless. He shook his fists in rage. He waved his vines in anger. He shouted:

"Drat and darn and fiddle de fum,
Where'd this rafty guy come from?"

But Jack could not enter the water. He stood on the shore glaring angrily with hate-filled holes-for-eyes as the river swept Curious and Midnight and Wartle and Winky away and away.

Poor Mad Tom poled downstream, far away from Jack. And the two horses watched until the lights of Jack's eyes disappeared altogether. And then and only then did they turn to Poor Mad Tom.

Curious was very curious.

"You're a human," he said in amazement.

"Quite right," said the boy, nodding. "Poor Mad Tom is human. Or mostly so."

He looked at his own hands, as if seeing them for the first time.

This made Wartle nervous, because up until this point he'd had the monopoly on hands. So he waved his own digits frantically to remind Curious of their value.

"Are you a *young* human?" asked Curious. He thought Tom looked about two in horse terms, which you know would place him around twelve for a human, but he wasn't sure.

"Is Poor Mad Tom young?" asked Poor Mad Tom. "He was young once. Long, long ago. How long he couldn't say. Poor Mad Tom feels as though he has been young forever."

Well, that was weird. Curious whispered out the side of his mouth to Midnight. "Why does he talk like that?" he asked Midnight. "Why does he call himself Tom? Can't he say 'I' and 'me'? Or is that how humans talk?"

"No," replied Midnight. "He talks like that because he's mad."

"When I get mad, I don't talk like that," said Curious. "I don't walk around saying 'Curious is angry. Grrrr, Curious.'"

"Not *mad* mad," explained Midnight. "Mad as in crazy."

"Oh," said Curious. He stepped a pace back from Tom. Poor Mad Tom laughed.

"Don't fear Poor Mad Tom," said the boy. "Tom hurts no living thing. But especially Tom will not hurt a unicorn. Not one who was plucked from the world and brought here just as Tom was."

"You were brought here?" asked Curious.

"Aye," said Tom. "Once Tom was a wee little lad with a mum and a da. But Tom liked to wander in woods. Too far from home Tom wandered. And that's when he saw her. And she saw Tom. She was so beautiful. And Tom was a pretty lad in his way. Or pretty enough. She took Tom, off to her palace, to be her servant and her jester, her pet and her toy."

"Do you mean you were abducted?" asked Curious. "Who took you?"

"She of all the flowers. It was the fairy queen that took Tom all those years ago," said Tom.

"What? No!" said Curious, who couldn't believe such

a thing. "Not the fairy queen. You must mean some other queen, some queen of the Wicked Fairies."

"No, Tom means the queen of the Court of Flowers. Tom knows it well. Many a long year he spent there too, until finally she had used up all the fun in him. Then she was bored with Tom, and what was left of Tom she cast out."

"She wouldn't," said Curious. "The fairy queen is a good queen. She saved the unicorns. She doesn't abduct children. And she doesn't throw them out of her palace. Why would she?"

Poor Mad Tom shrugged.

"She was older than Tom then. Perhaps now that she's younger than Tom she's not so interested."

Older first, then younger than Tom? This didn't make any sense to Midnight, and probably not to you. But Midnight knew Tom, and she was used to the weird things he said from time to time. The look she gave Curious said, "See, I told you he was crazy, but he's saving us."

But the look was wasted because Curious wasn't paying attention to Midnight.

"No, no, no," he said. "You must be mistaken, Tom. The fairy queen *saved* all the unicorns. She's a good queen. She has marshmallow parties, and she protects us from human hunters and Wicked Fairies."

"Tom knows what Tom knows," said Tom. "And the

Fair Folk are only good when it suits them. And the goodest they can be isn't really good, not good enough."

"No," said Curious. "I have a Scientific Mind. If the fairy queen is good, then she couldn't have done these things. So you must have met another fairy queen, who wasn't good. Not my fairy queen, who only does *good* things."

Tom regarded Curious with sad eyes.

"Tom thinks your friend is as mad as Tom. Perhaps more so," he said to Midnight. "At least Tom sees what's in front of him."

"He's not my friend," Midnight replied, just as Curious said, "I'm not mad."

Tom didn't look convinced.

"Then why do you wear a horseshoe on your head?" he asked.

"A horseshoe?" asked Curious. "Is that what this thing is?"

But then Wartle yelled, "Fishy, fishy, fishy!" and leapt from Curious's back.

Everyone turned to see what had caught his attention.

It was, as you might have guessed, a fish.

But a really large fish. And a special fish.

It was swimming alongside the raft. Then it stuck its head out of the water and it spoke.

That's right. The fish *spoke*.

"Faraway cows have long horns," it cried.

"What?" said Curious and Midnight together, as they had never seen a talking fish.

"A good start is half the work," said another fish, swimming up with a splash beside the first.

"If you're looking for a friend without a fault, you will be without a friend forever," said a third.

"Don't mind them," said Poor Mad Tom. "These are the Salmon of Wisdom. It's said eating them will make one wise, but they are terrible hard to catch."

Terrible hard to catch they might be, but that didn't deter our puckle. Wartle liked fish, whether they talked or not. He reached into the water and made a grab.

The fish leapt away.

"A kind word never broke a tooth!" it yelped as it leapt.

Wartle jumped after it. And he would have landed in the river, too, had Curious not chomped his little red jerkin with its shiny black buttons in his teeth.

Wartle struggled over the water.

"Fishy, fishy, fish!" he cried.

But the Salmon of Wisdom were swimming away.

One glanced back and offered a final bit of advice.

"He who lies down with dogs gets up with fleas," the fish said.

Then they were gone.

It was just as well, because something nasty was taking their place in the water.

Two somethings, actually. With a third terrible something on their backs.

Yes, the kelpies had returned. And they were making a beeline—or I suppose I should say they were making a kelpie-line—straight toward Poor Mad Tom's raft.

But they weren't any happier about it than our two horses were. Because the kelpies didn't have a choice.

No, they were bitted and bridled just like the new mysterious night mare had been. Ropey pumpkin vines twined around them like green reins, held in the dusty fists of two tattered gloves.

And a figure stood upon the backs of the unhappy kelpies, one foot on each.

Jack o' the Hunt had returned!

⚜ 15 ⚜

IS THAT A REALLY BIG SWAN WITH A GIANT ROSE ON TOP?

"What are we going to do? What are we going to do?"

Curious ran back and forth across the small space of the raft. He had never been *on* the water before, and only *in* the water once. And he didn't want to go into it again.

"Stop rocking the boat!" said Midnight, who was beginning to snort fire as her panic grew.

"Well, don't you burn it down!" said Curious. "Then where would we be?"

Pumpkin Jack sang out:

"In the drink

Where you will sink."

"I wasn't asking you!" shouted Curious.

"Have no fear, horses," said Tom, "for the fairy folk have never once set foot upon Poor Mad Tom's raft."

This was true. Indeed, Curious and Midnight saw that although Jack was very close now, almost close enough to hop onto the raft, he didn't. He stayed put upon the backs of the kelpies.

And the way he scowled and grimaced and glowered, it seemed that Jack wasn't very happy about it either.

But before Curious, Midnight, and Poor Mad Tom could feel anything approaching relief, Jack snapped his fingers on both his hands and two large pumpkins rose up behind his shoulders, swaying on their vines like the heads of fat orange cobras. Jack thrust his hands forward and the pumpkins shot forward.

They sailed through the air, striking Poor Mad Tom's raft.

Poom! Poom!

The two pumpkins splattered their messy orange guck all over the raft. It was gross. It looked like someone had thrown up a really messy upchuck. But also, it set the raft a-rocking. And maybe one or two of the planks of wood looked like they had been shaken loose.

Jack snapped again. More pumpkins flew.

Poom! Poom! Poom!

"Oh, yuck!" cried Curious. He wasn't used to being dirty, and while all new experiences should be beneficial to the Scientific Mind, still this one wasn't very fun.

Midnight could handle the muck and the yuck a little bit better, being a night mare and not a unicorn, but she knew they had other problems.

"He's tearing up the raft!" she shouted.

"Poor Mad Tom will fix it," cried Tom, and the boy pulled a hammer from a basket and began rushing about his craft. He drew nails from his pocket, and he drove them into the wood, hammering the planks back in place.

Bang! Bang! Bang!

But . . .

Poom! Poom! Poom!

Pumpkins came faster and the raft broke apart more quickly than Tom could repair it. In the water, the kelpies laughed. They might not like being ridden very much, but they would enjoy the chance to drown these two pesky ponies. Oh, yes, they would.

But Curious was watching the nails. He'd never seen such devices. And he was Curious, after all. So he took one in his teeth, and he set it on the wood. He raised his hoof.

"Not that way," said Tom, because Curious had set the nail upside down. "You'll drive it into your hoof."

Tom took the nail and turned it around, showing Curious that the point went into the wood.

Curious stomped on the nail hard and drove it into the plank.

Then he took more nails in his teeth and stomped on them as well. Midnight saw and joined in.

But *Poom! Poom! Poom!* went the pumpkins.

Tom and the horses were getting tired. The pumpkin fairy wasn't. Or at least he didn't show it.

And for all their stomping and hammering, the raft was still coming apart. Things were getting quite wobbly on the River Restless. And they were going to get worse.

Only that's when the music sounded.

Rich, loud, beautiful notes piping through the air.

Sailing on the river. Coming toward them.

A three-headed swan.

That's right. Three heads.

It was the biggest swan you ever saw. As big as a ship, because it was a ship. On its back was a giant rose made of crystal, as large as a house.

The great glass petals were all curled up, like a flower at night, but they were opening now.

Someone was standing in the rose. A bunch of someones.

They shined, they glowed, they radiated light. And one shone the brightest of all.

"It's *her,*" said Curious, smiling in awe. Which is to say respect, but also fear and wonder.

"Her?" said Midnight. She turned to Curious, who had that dopey "we're saved" adulation on his face. And she turned to Tom, who had taken a knee, but didn't look quite as happy. And she guessed who was coming just as Curious explained.

"Her," said the unicorn. "The fairy queen."

"Her?" said Midnight, straining her eyes to see. "Do you mean behind the little girl?"

"Um, no," said Curious, embarrassed by Midnight's remark. "She is the little girl. That's the queen of the Court of Flowers. Queen Titania."

"Oh," said Midnight, who didn't understand.

I bet you don't either.

I bet you were expecting someone beautiful and golden.

Well, Titania was beautiful and golden.

She just looked to be about five years old.

Now, don't be fooled. Queen Titania wasn't five. Or fifty-five. Or even five hundred and five. She was way older than that. Older than the world. Older than time. She wasn't even a creature of time at all.

But however old she might be or not be, she was very, very, very powerful.

So she could look however she wanted.

And lately, she wanted to look like a child. Which meant that all the fairies in her court had to change their appearances too. Because no one could look older than the queen.

So they were all five, or slightly younger, because she had to be the oldest.

And the thing about looking five is that sometimes you acted five too.

So Titania stamped her feet and puffed out her cheeks in exasperation.

"Jack, Jack, Jack," she said. "Naughty Jack. Chasing one of my unicorns."

"Jack didn't think that you would mind.
This unicorn had left its kind.
And as you know Jack has a need,
To ride upon a burning—"

"Shut up, Jack," said the queen. Which wasn't a very queenly thing to say. But she was angry. "Go back to your wicked woods."

She clapped her hands. The three-headed swan flipped a giant webbed foot, and a wave rose up and swept Jack across the River Restless, depositing him on the far shore.

Curious wondered what Jack had been about to say. What rhymed with "need"?

But he didn't have much time to ponder, because a crystal staircase was forming from the flower petals down to the edge of Tom's raft. Titania descended the staircase, followed by her fairy court.

But when she tried to set a glass-slippered foot on the raft, she yelled, "Ouch!" and drew back.

She snarled for a moment, paused, and smiled sweetly.

"Tom," she said.

"Yes, mum?" Poor Mad Tom replied.

"We see you're still using nails in your boat," she said.

"They hold the boat together, mum," the boy explained.

"They burn our feet," said the queen. "You don't want our feet to burn, do you, Tom?"

"No, mum. But the boat is my home."

"It doesn't have to be," said the queen. And she put on her most endearing smile. "You could come back to the palace with us."

"The palace, mum?" said Tom. A look of fear filled his face.

"Yes," said the queen. "You liked it there, didn't you? Didn't I always put you back together again after I took you apart?"

"What does she mean?" Midnight whispered to Curious. But maybe she whispered a little bit too loud, because the queen scowled at her.

"Oh, look. A little black horsey. You're like a shadow that doesn't know to hide from the sun. Shall I shine my light on you and brighten you up, little horsey?"

"This is Midnight," said Curious hastily. "She saved my life. *Several times.*"

"Did she, now?" said the queen. "Well, we've returned the favor."

She nodded to one of the three swan heads. It reached forward with its beak and plucked Midnight right off the boat, lifting her into the air.

Midnight kicked and struggled as she found herself higher in the sky than she had ever been.

"Stop squirming," said another swan head. "You're all slippery with pumpkin guck. You don't want us to drop you now, do you?"

Midnight was deposited right onto the crystal petal platform. She stood there on shaky legs, dripping pumpkin goop, looking around nervously at all the childish fairies.

The queen marched up the staircase.

"What an ugly little pony you are," she said.

Then she called to the swan heads looming over them.

"Well, what are you waiting for? Bring the other two as well."

A swan head plucked Curious off the raft, lifting him high into the air. As he swung in the bird's beak, the horseshoe slid from his horn and clattered to the floor of the raft. Curious had a nagging feeling he should have tried to catch it. But too late. It was gone.

At least for now.

Then another swan head reached for Poor Mad Tom, its beak opening wide. But before it could capture him, the boy ducked and held his nails aloft. The swan head hovered above him, as if it was afraid to approach any closer.

Curious thought this was most curious. They were just nails, after all. And yet the queen had complained about them.

"Tom," she said, stamping her foot. "Come aboard my boat."

"Thank you, mum," said Tom in a very polite voice, "but I must decline your hospitality."

The queen gave a little pout. "Don't you want to see all the changes I've made to my palace?"

"I'm sure they're wonderful, mum," said Poor Mad Tom. "But it's the changes you might make to me I'm rather worried about."

"Oh, Tom," said the queen with a sigh. "Don't be like that. You know, we always put something in you in place of whatever we took away."

Curious and Midnight saw Tom quake a little at this, but then the boy seized on the queen's words.

"That's just it, mum," he said. "My raft has lost parts too. I've got to put it back together now. It needs fixing, you know."

"Fine," said the queen with a little stamp of her little foot. "Be that way. I have other toys to play with now anyway."

She waggled her fingers and the swan flipped its webbed foot again. Poor Mad Tom was nearly capsized as his broken raft was caught in a large wave and sent bobbing wildly down the River Restless.

Curious and Midnight were alone with the not-children fairies and their childlike queen. She strode up to them and stroked Curious's neck.

"There, there, little pony," she said. "You're safe now." Her eyes were adoring. But they held a selfish little twinkle.

Then she turned to Midnight, her hand poised to touch the night mare. Midnight stiffened. The fairy queen was no friend to the creatures of the Whisperwood.

"Little wicked horsey," said the queen, "I bet you have a story to tell. Shall I make you tell it?"

16

MAYBE THINGS ARE FINALLY GOING TO BE OKAY . . .

"Tell us your story," the queen said. "The story of the ugly little pony."

Well, that wasn't nice, was it? Normally Midnight wouldn't stand for it. But she was on a strange ship, in a strange crystal flower, surrounded by strange and powerful fairies. She was really very out of her element. And somehow Curious had been separated from her.

Midnight saw him a little ways off, amid a cluster of

smiling childlike fairies who seemed excited to play with a unicorn. The rest of the court fairies were milling around tables piled high with sweets, stuffing their faces with cupcakes and marshmallow treats, sugared rose petals, and bowls of shaved and flavored ice. But all the fairies perked up at the queen's words.

"Ooooh, a story," the not-children called. "Tell us a story! Tell us a story!"

"Story?" said Midnight. "There's no story."

"No story? Boo!" jeered the not-children. "Boo! Hoo! Boo!"

"Of course there is a story," continued the queen. "There is always a story. Everything is a story. Tell us, little shadow mare, why are you on a boat on the River Restless with one of my unicorns? What nasty thing were you planning to do to him?"

"Nothing," said Midnight. "I wasn't doing anything nasty."

"I find that hard to believe," said the queen. "I don't like hard things."

This made Midnight feel quite put out.

"I don't care what you believe," she said. And all the not-children gasped. They weren't used to anyone talking back to the Queen of Flowers.

"In fact, I was saving him," continued Midnight.

"Saving him?" said the little queen. She laughed a high, childish laugh. "You're an ugly little liar."

"I am not," said Midnight.

"Liar, liar, hooves on fire," taunted the queen.

"Stop it," said Midnight. But actually her hooves were on fire now. She stomped angrily and a little jet of flame shot out across the deck of the swan boat.

Several of the child fairies jumped away at this, but the queen didn't even blink.

Then a cupcake sailed through the air and smashed Midnight in the flank. The queen turned an angry eye in the direction it had come from.

"Who threw that?" she demanded.

The not-children looked at their feet and didn't answer.

"Who was it?" said the queen.

One of the swan heads suddenly dipped to their level.

"It was the Duchess of Daisies," the swan head said.

"Stupid bird," said a little not-child with daisies in her hair.

"I am not," said the swan. "I'm very smart."

"Anyway," the Duchess of Daisies continued, "it was only because Baron Buttercup told me to."

"You tattletale!" hollered a little not-boy who was clearly the baron. "I'll get you for this!" He snatched a chocolate cupcake off the table and hurled it at the duchess.

It missed.

And struck the Marquis of Marigolds.

He grabbed an entire tray of marshmallow custards and threw them into the air.

The Prince of Primrose and Lady Lilac got the worst of it. The prince began to cry, but the lady grinned like a maniac and yelled, "Food fight!"

"Food fight?" said the first swan head.

"Yes, food fight!" said the second. Then the head snatched up the bowl of shaved ice and upended it over a group of not-children.

"Phbtttttt!" went the third swan head, blowing a raspberry. Then it threw some real raspberries.

Midnight ducked and dodged as the creamy confections flew through the air.

"Watch it!" said Curious. But anytime he got splattered, his shiny coat just sloughed off the sweets in seconds. By the moons, he was irritating!

Meanwhile, Wartle took the occasion to poke out from Curious's mane, where he had been hiding from the queen—remember, she didn't like puckles very much—to snatch sweets as they flew by. And occasional marshmallows.

"Gobble, gobble, gobble," said Wartle happily.

"Stop it! Stop it! Stop it!" yelled the queen.

She stomped her feet and shook her fists.

But things didn't really stop.

Not until a big creamy pie caught her in the face.

Then you could have heard every one of the not-children's hearts beat. If they'd had hearts. Which I don't think they did.

Everyone waited to see what the fairy queen would do.

She stuck out a tongue and licked at her cheek.

"I would have preferred strawberry," she said.

Then she waved her hand and all the sticky sweets flew from everyone's faces and clothing and from the floor and from the railings and banisters and from the swan's feathers. And it all went right back onto the table and reformed into all the desserts that were there before, and maybe even a few new ones. And everyone was clean.

Well, everyone but Midnight. Midnight was still sticky and covered in goo.

"I apologize for my courtiers," said the queen to the two horses. "The problem with looking like children is that everyone decides to act like them too. But never mind, here we are."

Curious and Midnight saw that the swan boat had stopped on the bank of the River Restless. A little ways offshore there was a wood. But not a nasty and gloomy wood like the Whisperwood. The Willowood was a green and golden wood without any underbrush or prickly thorns or dangerous creatures at all. A wood where the golden light of the sky never failed to shine between the tree limbs, and it was always bright and sunny.

"There you go, uni-boonie," said the queen. "You're home. You'll find your herd frolicking at the Glen of the Golden Goose."

Curious was relieved to be home.

"You may thank me now," said the fairy queen.

"Um," said Curious.

"You're welcome," said the fairy queen.

"Er," said Curious.

"What is it?" said the fairy queen.

"Well, it's just . . . what about her?" Curious pointed a hoof at Midnight.

"What about her?" said the fairy queen.

"She needs to get home too."

"Home?" said the fairy queen.

"She did save me," said Curious.

"More than once," said Midnight.

"Oh," said the fairy queen, giving Midnight a look. "Well, very well, I'll take her home, then."

"You will?" said Curious and Midnight together.

"Of course I will. Now off you go," said the fairy queen.

"But . . ."

"Don't you trust me to do what I say?" Titania frowned.

"Away with you. I'll see your shadowy little friend is taken care of."

"If I could just come—" said Curious.

But then the rude swan head blew another raspberry and the middle swan head plucked him up in its beak and swung him over the side of the boat and deposited him somewhat-but-not-too-gently on the bank of the River Restless.

"Bye-bye," said the fairy queen, waving down at Curious on the shore. "You're a curious little unicorn. You must come visit me in my palace sometime."

"Wait, wait!" called Curious, but the swan boat didn't wait. In fact, it was busy swimming down the river. And Curious was soon alone.

"I guess that's over with," he said.

"Over with," agreed Wartle.

But then Curious's Scientific Mind noticed something.

The swan boat carrying the fairy queen, the court of not-children, and the night mare Midnight was going the wrong way. It wasn't traveling toward the Whisperwood and the home of the Curse.

The swan boat was heading to the fairy queen's castle!

17

OR IS SOMETHING NOT QUITE RIGHT HERE?

Midnight was starting to get suspicious.

More than a little suspicious, if we're being honest.

She could see that the swan boat was heading in the wrong direction. She knew it wasn't heading toward her home.

Plus, she didn't trust that little fairy queen further than she could kick her. When you came right down to it, Midnight didn't trust any fairy. It didn't matter if they were from the Court of Flowers or the Court of Thistles or the

Court of Ice Cream Sundaes. She knew better than to trust fairies.

But fairies were very, very powerful. Fairy queens doubly so. And they could be quick to anger. Even the good ones. If there really are good ones. You might find yourself shrunken to the size of a mouse or turned into a bullfrog or magicked into a strawberry pie. Or maybe something really unpleasant might happen.

Midnight didn't want to be any of those things. Not even the strawberry pie.

So while she was becoming more and more worried about where they were or weren't going, she hadn't spoken up. She was hoping the queen would tell her what was going on. But the queen had wandered off, leaving Midnight alone with the not-children. No one spoke to her. Not even the swans.

Midnight was feeling lonely now. She could hear faint music playing in the air, but she couldn't tell where it was coming from. And if she tried listening to it, it faded away and only came back when she stopped paying attention. It was unsettling. It made her feel queasy and unwelcome.

She trotted hesitantly around the boat. She peered at the tables of sweets to see if there was something she could eat. But the food looked too rich, too sugary, and not suitable for horses.

The not-children tittered and giggled behind her back.

She turned to confront them, but none of them would meet her eyes.

I wish Curious were still here, she thought. Then she realized how very wrong that thought was.

I wish I'd never met that stupid unicorn. Then I wouldn't be in this mess.

That felt right.

But she *was* in the mess.

And, really, she *did* wish Curious were there.

She found the queen.

She was sitting on a giant marshmallow cushion conjuring butterflies out of thin air. The queen twirled her fingers and sent the butterflies fluttering frantically in a tiny storm. Midnight felt sorry for them.

When the queen didn't look up, Midnight waited to see if Titania would notice her.

"Excuse me," said Midnight. And then she said it again. "Excuse me."

"Your Majesty," replied the queen.

" 'Your Majesty'?" she repeated. "I'm not a queen."

Now the fairy queen did look up.

"No, of course you're not. You a queen? Don't be ridiculous. I meant you're supposed to say, 'Excuse me, Your Majesty.' Everything you say to me needs to have 'Your Majesty' at the end of it."

Titania wrinkled her nose and narrowed her eyes as if noticing Midnight for the first time.

"You're that ugly little pony that was with the curious unicorn, aren't you?" she said. "What are you still doing on my swan boat?"

Midnight was taken aback.

"You were giving me a ride home," she said.

"Your Majesty," said the fairy queen.

"What?"

"You were giving me a ride home, Your Majesty. You're supposed to end all your sentences with 'Your Majesty.'"

When Midnight didn't speak, the queen sighed.

"Was I really? A ride home?" she said. "I can't imagine what you'd want to go there for. The Whisperwood is such a dreadful place, full of so many dark things even nastier than you are."

It actually was. But Midnight was confused and offended by this. Of course she wanted to go home.

"But that's where the Curse is," she said.

"Well, I don't see why they'd want to be there," said the queen, as if the Curse had any choice. Then she swooshed her hand in the air, and all the butterflies were blown away.

"Anyway," said the queen, rising from her marshmallow. "I have a better idea. Why don't I show you my palace first?"

"Your palace?" said Midnight. She glanced around at the crystal rose petals rising around them. "I thought this was your palace."

"Oh, this?" said the queen in a dismissive voice. "No, this is just the deck of my swan boat. The palace of the Court of Flowers is ever so much bigger and much more impressive. There's nothing like it in the Whisperwood or anywhere. Not even the castle of the Court of Thistles. You really must see it."

Midnight knew she was on dangerous ground. She remembered how reluctant Poor Mad Tom had been to return to the palace.

"Thank you," she said. "But I really need to get home. My mother will be worried about me. And also . . ."

Her voice trailed off. She realized that she needed to find a way to fix the Silent Stones. Or else the Curse was going to have a very hard time sleeping through the night, what with all the Fairy Creatures trying to eat them.

"No, no, no," said the queen, rising and striding toward the front of her swan boat. "I insist. You must come and be my guest at the palace. And you'll be the first ugly little night mare ever invited, so that will make you special. Don't you want to be special?"

"I'm sorry," said Midnight. "But I have to say no." She looked over the crystal railing of the deck, wondering if she could survive a jump to the water below. And if she could survive the water afterward. There were still kelpies in the River Restless. Kelpies who were very mad at Midnight.

"No?" said the fairy queen. "What a funny word that is when someone else says it. No, you will be my guest. For as long as I like. Which will be no sooner than until I hear your story and no later than forever."

"I told you," said Midnight. "There's no story."

"Oh, I think you are full of plenty of stories," said the queen. "And full of something else too."

The queen climbed the crystal deck railing so that she could look Midnight in the eye. Then her little hand darted into Midnight's ear. Midnight jumped away, but the queen's small fist now held an Absorbing Orb with a wispy wood wink glowing inside.

"Starting with the story of where you got this," Titania said.

Midnight was amazed. She didn't know when Wartle had put the Absorbing Orb back in her ear. But obviously he had.

She looked at the Absorbing Orb in the queen's little hand.

"I don't know what that is," said Midnight.

"I don't know what that is, *Your Majesty*," replied the queen. "Everything needs to end with 'Your Majesty.' Even lies."

☙ 18 ☙

A BLESSING OF UNICORNS

"I have returned," said Curious. He had found his herd in the Glen of the Golden Goose, just as Queen Titania had promised.

The glen was a big wide-open area deep in the Willowood where the Blessing of Unicorns mostly lived. It was called the Glen of the Golden Goose for a very good reason.

A big golden goose mostly lived there too.

The golden goose had hatched from a golden egg—what else would she hatch from? She was three times the size of a regular goose. She was very fond of ice cream. And she was made of solid gold.

Apart from that, however, she was just a goose like any other. She mostly spent her days walking around her glen honking until someone fed her a treat.

It was a little noisy, but she was shiny and pretty. And shiny and pretty went a long way with unicorns.

What didn't go very far with unicorns was Curious. They were too busy frolicking to notice him.

"I'm back," he said again.

"Oh," said a unicorn named Harmonyhoof. "Were you gone?"

"Yes," said Curious. "I've been gone all night."

"That's wonderful," said a unicorn named Audacity. "There's going to be a marshmallow-eating contest this afternoon. You're just in time."

"But . . . weren't you worried about me?" asked Curious.

"Why would we worry?" asked Harmonyhoof.

"Because I was nearly drowned by kelpies, and then I was stranded on the other side of the River Restless."

"You were on the *other* side?" said a unicorn named Dawnsparkle. "Was it terrible? Was it horrible?"

"Well, yes and no," said Curious. "It was very exciting. But . . . didn't Grace tell you about it?"

All the unicorns blinked at him. Blink, blink, blink.

Curious looked around for his friend Grace.

"She must have told you," said Curious. "She ran off sometime after the kelpies attacked. I think after I swam to the other side. She went for help. At least, I thought she went for help."

"Oh," said Harmonyhoof. "Well, that explains it. Grace isn't here."

"Where is she?" asked Curious.

"Somewhere else," she said.

"But *where*?" said Curious. "What if she's in trouble?"

"Was she on the other side of the River Restless too?" asked Harmonyhoof.

"No," said Curious.

"Then I don't see how she could be in any trouble. All the trouble stays on that side. I really wouldn't worry about her."

"No," said a newcomer. "Curious needn't worry about Grace. He has enough to worry about for himself."

It was Goldenmane, the head of the Blessing. The biggest, brightest, goldenest unicorn around. And while Goldenmane always looked very handsome, right then he didn't look very happy.

"Did I hear correctly that you were on the *other* side of the River Restless?" asked Goldenmane.

"Well, yes . . . ," began Curious.

"The *other* side," repeated Goldenmane. "*Their* side?"

"Yes," said Curious. "You see, I was chasing a wispy wood wink, to learn about magic, and I fell in the river. But it's okay, because Midnight saved me."

"Midnight?"

"She's a night mare."

Around him, Harmonyhoof, Dawnsparkle, and Audacity all gasped. That was the proper reaction, so Goldenmane gave them an approving nod. Then he glared at Curious.

"A night mare?" said Goldenmane. "*Saved* you? Why would a night mare save you? That isn't possible."

"That's what I thought too," said Curious. "But guess what? It turns out that we're wrong about them. At least about some of them."

"Some of them? You've met more?"

"Well . . . all of them, I think," said Curious. "The whole of the Curse."

Gasp, went Harmonyhoof, Dawnsparkle, and Audacity.

"Curious," said Goldenmane, "I think you had better tell me everything."

So Curious did. All of it. He was very excited. After all, he had seen and learned a lot, and his Scientific Mind was eager to share.

Unfortunately, Goldenmane didn't have a Scientific Mind. He didn't view things the way Curious did. Not at all.

"Curious," said Goldenmane. "You are lucky to be alive. I am just glad our wonderful fairy queen rescued you from the clutches of that Creature of Wickedness."

"That's not exactly how it happened," said Curious. "And anyway, Midnight is not a 'Creature of Wickedness.' Not really."

Curious felt bad. Because he realized a "Creature of Wickedness" is exactly what he'd called her. More than once.

"She is most certainly a Creature of Wickedness," said Goldenmane. "Didn't she lead you deeper into the Whisperwood when she told you she was leading you out? Didn't she lead you into a trap at the Silent Stones? Weren't you nearly killed time and again? No, it's a miracle you survived. In fact, I think it's only because so *many* different creatures were trying to kill you that none of them succeeded. Their efforts canceled each other out. Yes, that must be it."

"But Midnight—"

"Is back where she belongs."

"I'm not sure about that," said Curious. "I think she might be in trouble."

"In trouble?" said Goldenmane. "She *is* trouble. Night mares are evil, twisted creatures. Unicorns are good, pure creatures. That is the reason we live in the Willowood and they live in the Whisperwood. Their kind and our kind can never get along."

"But we *did* get along. At least, we were starting to. I'm sure if we had more time—"

"Enough," interrupted Goldenmane, stamping a hoof. "I am trying to be clear, but you are not getting it. Let me be as direct as possible. From now on, you are forbidden from ever crossing the River Restless again. You are forbidden from even going *near* the River Restless. And you are most certainly forbidden from ever, ever mentioning this 'Midnight' Creature of Wickedness again."

And with that, Goldenmane trotted away.

Curious looked at Harmonyhoof, Dawnsparkle, and Audacity. But they wouldn't meet his eye. Instead, they cantered off to different parts of the glen.

"Well, that didn't go very well," said Curious.

19

MIDNIGHT IN THE PALACE

"You're going to want to watch this," said the fairy queen.

Midnight stood beside her at the bow of the boat. The swan began to turn toward the shore.

"Maybe I should get off?" asked Midnight. The queen didn't answer.

The swan stretched out its two great wings to either side.

And with a flutter and a flap, it rose into the air.

"We're flying!" cried the night mare.

"Obviously," said the queen, but she was smiling quite broadly now.

"But," said Midnight, "if you can fly, why did you need to sail in the river at all? Couldn't you just fly over it?"

Queen Titania rolled her queenly eyes at this.

"What's the point of a swan boat if it never goes in the water? It wouldn't be much of a boat then, would it? A swan that wasn't a boat would just be a swan, and what's so special about that?"

Midnight was going to say something about the three heads, but she was captivated by the view. All the meadows and woods she'd never seen before. Because, of course, night mares weren't normally allowed here. She was amazed. She was angry. Because everything was more beautiful even than she'd imagined. And then she saw Queen Titania's palace.

What a palace!

I don't know how many palaces you've ever seen but even if you've seen a dozen, still you've never seen a palace like this. Oh, no!

Maybe you've been to Uskiri and seen the Summer Court of Shambok the Spectacular, with its famous flowing fountains. Well, this was more impressive.

Maybe you've been to Araland, to the Emerald Fortress of Queen Ulla. Well, this was shinier and shimmerier.

I don't care if you've been to the Pyramid Palace of the Phantasmagorical Pharaoh of Neteru. That doesn't hold a candle to this. Oh, no.

The palace of Queen Titania looked like a castle made of frozen sunlight—all the towers and turrets and parapets and walkways and bulwarks and whatever else a castle has, each rendered in gleaming, translucent golden perfection.

Actually, when you think about it, it looked a lot like dried honey.

"What—what is it made of?" asked Midnight.

"It's the Palace of Amber," said the queen, looking very pleased. "So, um, naturally, it's made of amber."

As they approached the gleaming yellow-brown turrets and towers of the Palace of Amber, big yellow-brown doors midway up the walls suddenly opened.

The Swan Boat went into a dive. Then it tucked its wings in and, with a few awkward flops of its flippers, landed in a big interior space.

The crystal rose petals folded themselves into crystal steps. The fairy queen and the not-children all ran giggling and squealing into the palace, where tables piled with more sweets and treats awaited them.

The queen looked over her shoulder to spy Midnight still hesitating atop the steps. "Welcome to the Court of Flowers, I suppose," she said.

Then the steps rippled and flowed under Midnight's hooves. The night mare stumbled, but she couldn't resist being swept right along, down the steps and onto the floor.

"Good luck, kid," said a swan head. Then the whole bird turned around and took to the air. The great doors to the palace shut with a loud boom.

Midnight noticed that there were flowers embedded inside the amber of the doors. And in the walls. In the floors. Roses, lilies, and tulips. Sweet peas, carnations, and orchids. Sunflowers, silver bells, and cockle shells. All trapped below the amber. They were beautiful. They were eternally preserved. But also eerie.

All the flowers in the Court of Flowers are dead, thought Midnight.

She had a sudden image pop into her head of herself, trapped inside a block of the honey-colored stone, her fires frozen mid-flicker. She felt an unaccustomed chill. Brrrr . . .

But she felt even worse when the queen glared at her again. Titania raised her little hand, palm upward. She snapped the fingers of her other hand and suddenly the Absorbing Orb appeared in her grasp.

"Remember this, horsey?" said the queen.

Midnight gulped. She nodded.

"I should think so. You had it in your ear. You had one of *my* Absorbing Orbs in *your* nasty ear."

"I d-don't have hands . . . ," stammered Midnight.

The queen wrinkled her nose.

"What do hands have to do with anything?"

"For carrying . . ."

"Look, horsey," the queen said. "Someone has been sneaking into my palace and taking my Absorbing Orbs. It's been going on for a long while now, and I'm getting tired of it. They're *mine*. Do you understand me? Mine!"

That was confusing. Midnight was pretty sure Curious had only taken a single orb.

"You're missing more than one?" she asked.

"Yesssss," said the queen, drawing her anger out in an obnoxious, exaggerated way.

"What do you do with Absorbing Orbs anyway?" asked Midnight.

"Light the palace with them at night, of course," said the queen. "And now whole rooms and corridors are all dark. I don't like the dark. So now I want to know, how did a horrible little horsey like you get my Absorbing Orb? And where are all the others?"

"I don't know anything about the others," said Midnight. "I don't even know about this one."

"I find that very unlikely," said the queen. "I know about you night mares. You stick together, and you stay in your Whisperwood where you belong. But here you are, traveling on Tom's raft, away from your hex, or jinx, or whatever you call it."

"Curse," said Midnight.

"Don't you dare," said the queen, cupping her hands to the sides of her head. "My young ears are too sensitive to hear it!"

Of course, she wasn't really young at all. She was just pretending at being young.

"No, you misunderstand," Midnight began to explain.

"No, I don't," said the queen. "I understand perfectly well. You're the one who has been crossing the river to steal my orbs. Now you tell me why, and where the other ones are, and you tell me *right now.*"

She stamped her foot, and a little flash of light shot through the amber.

"I haven't stolen anything," protested Midnight. "And I don't know anything about your other Absorbing Orbs. I only wanted the wink inside of it so I could control my fire."

Titania looked at the orb in her hand. For whatever reason, the wispy wood wink inside it had dimmed, so it's possible she didn't even see it.

"You can tell me now, or you can tell me later," said the queen.

"There's nothing to tell," insisted Midnight. In fact, she was so insistent that she shot a little blast of fire. But the queen wasn't fazed. She just stepped to the side and the fire flew past.

"'There's nothing to tell, *Your Majesty*,' you mean," she said. "Well, I think that after a night in my dungeon, you may change your mind."

She waved a hand then.

Midnight tried to leap away, but where she landed, the amber under her hooves grew soft. It was like thick goo. She couldn't lift her legs out of it. In fact, she was sinking, down, down into the thick, syrupy mush.

Midnight panicked. She started to thrash and buck. Her mane burned but her hooves were too glopped with goop. She pictured herself again trapped inside the amber forever.

"Help!" she cried, though she didn't know who would help her. In no time at all, she had sunk so low into the floor that the little queen was above her. Titania looked down at Midnight as she slipped away.

"Don't worry," said the queen as Midnight disappeared into the floor. "You'll like it in my dungeon. It's dark, just like you."

And then Midnight was swallowed up, and the floor became solid once again.

Midnight was gone.

20

CURIOUS'S CONUNDRUM

Curious had a conundrum.

On the one hoof, his ordeal was over if he wanted it to be. He was safely back on the right side of the River Restless. No kelpies trying to drown him. No festerlings trying to fester him. No night mares trying to stomp him. And no pumpkins trying to do whatever it was they were trying to do. He was safe. He was secure. A unicorn among unicorns. And that—he knew—was nothing to sneeze at.

On the other hoof, he had a growing suspicion that Queen

Titania was not taking Midnight home despite her promise to do so. Oh, she was a marvelous queen for unicorns—as long as you didn't mess up her parades or steal her Absorbing Orbs. But she probably wasn't a good queen for night mares, or anyone who came from the other side of the river.

On the third hoof, what did any of that have to do with him? He hadn't intended to cross the river, get chased by Jack o' the Hunt, and go to the Curse. A lot of that seemed to have been Midnight's fault. Why should he care about her anyway? She wasn't a unicorn. She was a night mare. A Creature of Wickedness. Goldenmane and Queen Titania were probably right: it was better that unicorns stay on their side and night mares stay on theirs.

The only problem was . . . Curious had one more hoof.

And on that hoof, he knew that it was Midnight who had saved him again and again. Midnight had been by his side when Grace had run off—and where was Grace anyway? Midnight had shared his interest in wispy wood winks. Oh, she wanted to eat it, not study it for scientific purposes, but she did make Plans, which were kind of like Experiments. He liked that she was going and doing and not sitting around eating marshmallows all day. Horses like Curious and Midnight, they were . . . well, they were . . . curious.

And that was the problem. He was always doing things the Blessing didn't like or agree with or even understand. He had to admit, he just wasn't like the other unicorns.

So maybe he didn't *have* to be like other unicorns.

If he wanted to make sure his friend was okay, he would. And if she was in trouble, he'd save her. And if she wasn't, what was the harm? The queen had invited him to the palace sometime, hadn't she? Sometime could be anytime.

Of course, it wouldn't do to tell the other unicorns what he was up to. They wouldn't understand. They might not even let him go. Curious waited until nightfall. And in the meantime, he pretended to be a unicorn just doing unicorn things. He fed the golden goose, and he even came in second place in the marshmallow eating contest.

Finally night came, and the unicorns settled down for bed.

The Blessing slept inside a large ring of mushrooms, a fairy ring. When you see one it means that fairies have danced upon the grass the night before. At the Glistening Isles, the ring never wilted. In fact, its mushrooms were quite large, shoulder high on a unicorn.

There was just one gap where the Blessing could slip in and out.

"Bedtime," said Goldenmane as Curious lingered by the gap.

"Right," said Curious. He pretended to yawn. "I'm probably tired after my horrible ordeal and all."

Goldenmane nodded, but the head of the Blessing must have been suspicious, because he lay down right across the exit.

Well, that was a problem.

But Curious wasn't daunted. Oh, no. He waited until Goldenmane looked asleep. Then he gathered himself and *one, two, three,* he jumped. It was a big jump for him, but he managed it. He sailed right over the red-and-white caps and landed on the grass on the other side. Then, checking to see he hadn't been spotted, Curious trotted into the Willowood.

By this time, the night was quite advanced. But a night in the Willowood is still glorious and bright. There were plenty of fireflies and crystal critters and pixies scattering their sparkling dust. It was everything a good fairy forest should be.

So off he went.

At least until someone behind him demanded, "Where are you going?"

Of course it was Goldenmane. He hadn't been asleep after all. He'd only been pretending.

"That way," said Curious, pointing with a hoof.

"Didn't I tell you—?" began Goldenmane.

"You told me to stay away from the River Restless," said Curious. "The River Restless is that way." And here he pointed with a hoof in the opposite direction.

"And I told you not to have anything to do with that night mare again."

"You told me not to mention her again. I haven't mentioned her. At least, not until you brought her up just now."

"Curious," said Goldenmane, "I am very disappointed in you. Don't disappoint me further."

"I'm just going to the palace," said Curious. "Queen Titania said she would take the night mare home. If she has, I'll come right back. And that will be the end of that."

Goldenmane shook his golden mane.

"Why should it matter what the queen chooses to do with the night mare creature?"

"Because she saved me," said Curious.

"I doubt that," said Goldenmane. "But if she did, she had her own twisted reasons."

"Yes," said Curious. "She said she saved me to prove she was better than we were."

"Well, that's absurd," said Goldenmane. "Unicorns are obviously better than night mares."

"Not if I stay here, we're not," said Curious. "If I stay here doing nothing, then we're considerably worse." And he trotted forward.

"Curious," called Goldenmane after him. "If you leave here tonight, we may not welcome you back."

Curious stopped then. He'd been in trouble before. Plenty of times. But this—being unwelcome in the herd? That was something else.

Goldenmane saw him hesitate.

"Think about it," the leader of the Blessing said. "All on your own. Without any other unicorns. You'd be alone, an outcast. And for what? A night mare! Ask yourself, is she really worth it?"

"I don't know," said Curious.

Goldenmane tossed his head in horsey triumph. He thought he'd won the argument.

"I don't know," repeated Curious. He gave a toothy grin. "But I'm curious to find out."

And with that, he galloped into the woods, heading toward the queen's palace and Midnight the night mare.

21

IT'S PROBABLY TIME FOR A BIG SECRET TO BE REVEALED

Midnight was in a proper dungeon.

Unlike the rest of Queen Titania's palace, the dungeon wasn't made of amber and frozen flowers. It was rock and stone, deep under the ground. Dark and dank and chilly. It was all the things that a dungeon should be.

It didn't look much like it was made by fairies. Probably it was built by those wild, blue-tattooed people who had lived on the Glistening Isles before they glistened. Before the Court of Flowers and the Court of Thistles came to chase them all away.

Midnight was in one of the dungeon cells now. It was a square room, hardly big enough for her to turn around in, with a ceiling so low her ears scraped against it when she perked them up.

And she had to perk them up, because the light was dim here, so she needed to hear what she could hear because she couldn't see what she could see.

Only, so far, all she could hear was that sort of empty nothing you would expect from a dungeon. Just her own nervous breathing. And the occasional drip, drip, drip of moisture seeping through the stones. Nothing else.

Midnight snorted a little flame. It flickered in the darkness, reflecting in the solid wall of amber that sealed her in.

Yes, amber. Because whatever door that had once locked people in this cell had been made of wood. And it had rotted away long ago.

So the queen made a door of amber to trap prisoners in their cell. It didn't have a knob or a latch. It simply appeared and disappeared as the queen commanded.

Midnight couldn't whisk it away. She didn't have that kind of magic.

She just had her fire.

Her wild, crazy, hard-to-control, unpredictable fire.

What good could that do her here, trapped in a small stone room behind a wall of amber?

She gave it a kick.

And hurt her hoof.

It was hard. Hard like stone.

She turned and gave it both back legs. Hard as she could.

And nearly knocked herself silly when she was propelled into the far wall.

She blew another burst of fire and studied the result.

It was undamaged. Smooth as brown glass.

So kicking wouldn't work.

She was frightened.

But as I've said before, fear didn't really last long inside Midnight.

Her fires were too hot. They were getting hot now, burning up all her fear and turning it to anger.

She blew another blast and saw herself reflected in the amber.

Fire. Amber.

Amber, hard like stone. Smooth like glass.

Would it heat like stone?

Or would it melt like glass?

Midnight's ears perked up.

She had an idea. It was a good one.

She just needed her fire.

A lot of fire.

She began to stomp. She snorted and neighed, anger stoking her flames.

And she began to burn, burn, burn.

She channeled that flame at the door.

Little tongues of fire were curling this way and that. It was hot. Blazing. In a very small space.

The door began to melt.

A little hole appeared right in the middle of the amber wall. The hole grew and grew.

It was working!

Midnight burned hotter and hotter.

Soon she had a hole in the doorway big enough she could step through it.

So she did.

Now, the smart thing would be to escape right away. Isn't that what you would do if you had just gotten out of a dungeon cell? That's what I'd do, I'm sure.

But this wasn't Midnight's Plan.

She wanted her wispy wood wink.

Instead of looking for a way *out,* she was looking for a way *up.*

She was going to find the place where the queen kept her Absorbing Orbs, and she was going to get the one with her wink in it. And then she was going to escape.

She heard something.

A kind of *clomp, clomp, clomp* sound.

Someone was coming. Oh, no! Midnight wasn't ready to be caught.

She ducked around a corner and hid as best she could. She waited for whoever was coming.

Clomp, clomp, clomp.

The clomping approached her corner.

The clomping rounded her corner.

The clomping arrived.

She leapt at the clomp maker.

"Ow!" screamed Curious as Midnight barreled into him.

"?!?!?!?!" replied Midnight as they tumbled and stumbled, their legs all tangly.

"!!!!!" he snorted in response.

Midnight and Curious struggled to separate and stand.

"What are *you* doing here?" they both said at once.

"I was looking for—" they both answered at once.

But then Curious said "you" just as Midnight started to say "the wispy wood wink," but she only got as far as "the wispy woo." She stopped, openmouthed.

"*You* were looking for *me*?" she said.

"Well, yes," said Curious. "Why wouldn't I be?"

"Why *would* you be?" she asked. "You were home. With your unicorns."

"I was home, yes, but, well, you weren't. Not in your home. I mean, I had to make sure you were all right, didn't I? I wasn't exactly sure the queen was taking you home straightaway. But if you're a guest of the court—"

"I'm not a guest!" Midnight interrupted. "I'm a prisoner. She put me in a dungeon."

"A dungeon?" repeated Curious. Now it was his turn to be surprised. "Are you sure it was a dungeon?"

"Of course I'm sure."

"Maybe you only thought it was a dungeon. Have you been in many dungeons before?"

"We're in a dungeon now!"

Curious looked around. Midnight had traveled a bit and here the walls were more amber than stone. They had some pretty flowers in them. He gave her a skeptical look.

"It's worse behind me," Midnight said. "Anyway, I need to keep moving. I need to get my Absorbing Orb—"

"You mean *my* Absorbing Orb."

"I think you promised it to me. If I got you home. And you are home. Anyway, I need that, and then I need to escape."

Curious gave her another skeptical look.

"I need to escape the rest of the way," she explained. "I'm out of the cell but not out of the palace. And the queen isn't going to just let me go."

"Why not?" said Curious.

Midnight fixed him with a fiery look.

"Someone has been stealing her Absorbing Orbs for a while now, and she thinks it's me."

"Oh," he said. "I'm sorry about that. Wait? Orbs? She's lost more than one of them?"

"A whole bunch, apparently," said Midnight.

"But I only took the one."

"Then who's been taking the others?" asked Midnight.

"I can't help you there," said Curious.

"Then if you don't mind," said Midnight, and she began to trot away.

"Wait," said Curious. "I've still got to help you escape."

"I've already escaped," said Midnight.

"Not all the way," Curious reminded her. That was a good point, and Midnight had to admit she was glad of the company.

They trotted on through the corridors and passages, peering into the rooms they passed. And they saw many strange things. Like a fountain of frozen wishes, a room where it rained indoors and upside down, and a song in a cage that might once have been stolen from a pretty enough lad. But no Absorbing Orbs with wispy wood winks inside them.

And then . . .

Footsteps. Echoing down the hallways.

And voices.

"One-two, one-two," said the voices.

Coming around the corridor were two leprechaun guards. Leprechauns were on generally friendly terms with the Court of Flowers, and the queen often employed them as guards and servants.

"Run," said Curious.

He and Midnight quickly ducked down a side passage.

"Were we seen?" asked Midnight.

"I don't think so," said Curious.

"Whew," said Midnight. But in her excitement, her fires suddenly blazed up.

"Hey, what's that light there?" called one of the leprechauns.

"Could be the glint of gold," said the other.

"Well, I saw it first," said the first leprechaun.

"Well, I saw it second," said the other.

Curious and Midnight had to run and hide and duck and swivel. There's not much that's more determined than a leprechaun on the hunt for gold. And although our horses stayed ahead of them, Midnight's fire blazed when she ran. So the light of her flames kept giving them away.

"It's over there! It's over here!" cried the leprechauns.

"Quit flaming!" hissed Curious.

"I flame when I run," said Midnight. "We can't not run."

"Then we have to hide," said Curious.

"Where?" said Midnight.

But suddenly, almost as if they'd asked for it to be there, the unicorn and night mare turned a corner, and found themselves facing a big, big wooden door. Two doors actually. Very ornately carved all over with flowers of every shape and size.

"And unicorns!" said Curious, who saw that unicorns adorned the left-side door.

"And . . . night mares!" said Midnight.

"Surely not!" said Curious. "Let me see."

But there they were. Horses with fiery manes and sparky hooves and smoke curling from their nostrils, all over the right-side door. And in the middle of the two doors, where the seam of their parting ran from top to bottom, they saw the strangest thing.

It was a horse, facing straight out at them, across the two doors. But every bit of horse on the left-side door was unicorn, and every bit of the right-side door was night mare.

"What does it mean?" Midnight asked.

"Why would the fairy queen have night mares on her door at all?" asked Curious. "She calls you ugly burning horsies. This is impossible."

Midnight glanced at the door. Something about it was

making her uneasy. Curious felt it too. The doors felt *heavy,* and *ominous,* and *strange.* They made you want to turn and run away.

But behind them came the sound of the leprechaun guards, laughing in their pursuit.

Despite the weird vibes coming off the doors, Curious and Midnight had no choice. They needed to hide, and fast.

They pushed against the doors and trotted into the room.

22

THE CROWN OF HORNS

Beyond the strange doors lay a very big chamber with a marble floor, high ceilings, and rows of wide columns. At one end, a carved oaken box sat on a plump red cushion on a dais.

And that was very curious.

But the other end of the chamber was curious too.

At the other end of the chamber was a mirror. A really big mirror. With an ornate silver frame. Two unlit wax candles in tall stands were placed on either side of the mirror.

The mirror was polished so well that it shone with its own light. Or maybe it had other reasons for shining.

"I'm guessing that mirror is magical," said Midnight. "I can't imagine there would be a mirror deep in a fairy queen's palace that wasn't."

"My Scientific Mind agrees," said Curious.

They trotted over to the mirror.

The silver frame was fashioned to look like twining vines. The shape of the vines seemed familiar to both of them.

"Ooooh," said Curious, stepping back.

"What is it?" asked Midnight.

"Don't you feel it?" he replied. "It feels . . . sick."

Midnight shook her head, tossing her mane.

"No," she said. "If anything, it feels kind of . . . homey."

"I don't like it. There's something not right about it," said Curious.

"I didn't like the door," said Midnight.

"Neither did I," said Curious. "But I like the mirror even less."

"Okay," said Midnight. "What about the box?"

They cantered over.

The oak of the box was stained a deep red. You could say it was a blood red, and you wouldn't be wrong. But whether it was stained with actual blood or not, let's not ask.

There was a latch on the lid.

Hooves weren't designed for latches.

"What do we do?" asked Midnight and Curious together.

"Hands!" shouted Wartle gleefully, popping up between them.

"Wartle?" said Curious. "Where did you come from?"

"Door," said Wartle.

"But we didn't see you when we came in," said Midnight.

"Not that door. That door." Wartle pointed.

Curious and Midnight looked where the puckle indicated and saw a small fairy door.

"Miss me?" said Wartle.

"Of course," said Curious, who hadn't actually thought about the puckle since returning to the Blessing. But he was glad of him now.

"You're just in time," Midnight said, who had thought about the puckle but hadn't missed him. "Can you open this latch?"

"Of course," said Wartle.

He approached the blood-red box, twiddling his fingers. Then he put his hands together and cracked his knuckles theatrically. *Crack-crack-crack-crack-crack!*

"Just get on with it," said Midnight.

Wartle huffed in an offended little voice.

He reached out a single finger and flicked the latch. Then he stepped back and took a bow.

Curious and Midnight trotted forward.

They each raised a hoof and placed it on either side of the lid.

"Together," Curious said.

They tipped it open.

The lid fell backward with a creak.

And a blazing silver light rose up from the box. It lit up their faces. It made them squint. Wartle jumped back a pace.

It took all their eyes a moment or three to adjust before any of them could see clearly again.

When they did, their mouths dropped open.

None of them could believe what they were seeing.

A crown sat on a red, velvety cushion.

The crown was partially made of silver.

It was beautifully wrought, a band of gleaming metal flowers.

And that was very nice.

But that wasn't the unbelievable part.

This was the unbelievable part:

The rest of the crown, all the pointing bits that rose from the silver flower band and stuck up—

—they were made from—

It's really too terrible to say, but here I go:

Twelve unicorn horns.

Twelve *unicorn* horns.

That's right.

Twelve unicorn *horns.*

The horns were all broken off at the base, as if they'd been sawn or cut or maybe even just ripped right from unicorn heads. Horns savagely stolen, fashioned into a crown.

It was horrifying.

Obscene.

It was . . .

A Crown of Horns.

"Why would the queen have this?" wondered Midnight.

Curious didn't answer. He couldn't answer.

Curious just shook his head. Back and forth. Back and forth. Like his Scientific Mind couldn't accept the total wrongness of what he was seeing.

This was what the Blessing had fled from.

This was what they thought they had escaped.

Their worst nightmare. And it was right here, in the fairy queen's palace.

Curious's mouth opened so wide you could hear his jaws groaning. His eyes popped so far they were in danger of falling out. The hairs of his mane even seemed to stand on end.

Midnight gave him a concerned look.

"Curious?" she said.

"No," he whispered. Then he said again, "No, no, no, no, no."

He began to stumble backward, moving away from the Crown of Horns like it might bite him.

"No, no, no, no, no."

"Curious," asked Midnight. "What's your queen doing with a crown made of unicorn horns?"

But Curious was still pacing backward. Still saying "no, no, no, no, no" and getting louder. He was like water working its way to a boil.

He backed all the way across the room until he bumped into the mirror on the other side.

The mirror wobbled on its stand. Then it settled.

Weirdly, though, the glass looked to Midnight like it was still wobbling.

Not wobbling. Rippling, like waves on a pond when someone tosses in a rock.

Suddenly, flames sprang to life on the two candles in their tall stands.

Now, you probably think that mirrors rippling magically and candles bursting to life by themselves couldn't be good. You're right. It wasn't good. Neither was what happened next.

An image began to form in the mirror.

Midnight watched the rippling and the flaming and the image, and she guessed what it meant.

"Curious," said the night mare, "someone is coming! We have to hide."

"No, no, no, no, NO!" said Curious.

"Hide, Curious, hide," urged Wartle.

"NO, NO, NO, NO, NO!" Curious was really boiling over now, and his shouts were getting louder and louder.

"Curious," said Midnight, "snap out of it. Someone is coming here. Through the mirror! We have to hide! Now!"

There wasn't any more time. If Curious wouldn't snap out of it on his own, Midnight would have to snap for him.

She ran forward and shoved Curious with her flank. She pushed him to the edge of the room, where the rows of wide columns stood.

Curious blinked at her. His eyes were panicked. But he saw her. And then he saw the mirror.

The image in the glass was really clear now.

It was a grinning orange image.

Of course it was. Oh, dear.

Curious finally understood.

"We have to hide," he said.

"That's what I've been telling you," said Midnight.

"Me too," said Wartle. "I've been telling you too."

Together, the two horses and the puckle ducked behind a column. They held their breath, and they peered at the mirror.

Two pumpkin vines, one on either side, broke the surface of the mirror like plants rising from a sideways pond.

They twisted in the air. It looked as though they were sniffing the room. Like hounds scouting for their master. Then, satisfied, they recoiled into the glass.

A moment later, Jack o' the Hunt stepped out of the mirror and into the chamber.

His tattered clothes flapped around him as if they were in a breeze. But there was no breeze here. How could there be? Maybe the breeze came from the mirror.

Vines stretched out from under his torn and dingy cape. They groped about the room like questing tentacles.

Even upset as he was, Curious had so many questions.

What were the vines looking for? What was Jack o' the Hunt doing here? How could the pumpkin fairy emerge from a mirror? And . . . had he done it before? What would the queen do if she found a Wicked Fairy sneaking into her home?

A pair of vines stretched all the way to the blood-red box. Careful not to touch the Crown of Horns, they tapped the edges of the box. Then they pulled away.

Jack raised his pumpkin head as if they'd alerted him. Then he walked swiftly to the dais.

He reached out a hand, poised above the Crown of Horns.

"Don't you dare touch that!"

The fairy queen had entered the room.

Curious was almost relieved. Queen Titania was here. Now Jack would be in trouble.

But Curious wasn't relieved. Because if he and Midnight were caught, they would be in trouble too.

"Not good, not good," said Wartle. He was right.

THE FAIRY QUEEN SHOWS HER TRUE COLORS

The unicorn and the night mare tried to keep as still as they could.

But they were curious.

They knew the queen couldn't possibly be happy to see Jack o' the Hunt invading her palace.

"He's going to get it now," whispered Curious.

Midnight nodded. She didn't like the fairy queen. But she wouldn't mind seeing Jack o' the Hunt "get it."

Both horses peered nervously around the column where they hid. They didn't want to be caught. But they very much wanted to know what would happen next. They wanted to see Jack get it.

But Jack didn't get it.

He didn't get it at all.

The fairy queen didn't raise a hand and blast him into pumpkin pulp.

She just stood there tapping her little foot. *Tap, tap, tap.*

Jack sighed, long and loud, very much for effect.

"I see your crown is nearly done.
And I must wonder, oh, what fun
You intend to spring upon our isle.
Why, even guessing makes me smile."

The pumpkin fairy turned a wide, nasty grin on the fairy queen, so wide that some wax from his candle ran down his pumpkin cheek like drool.

"You stay away from that," spat the queen. "It's not yours!"

Jack stretched out a tattered glove. His fingers were poised above the crown. He was clearly testing the queen's patience.

Titania stomped a little foot in frustration.

Purple energy shot out in all directions. It swept across the amber floor like a wave. When it reached Curious and Midnight, they had to jump to avoid it touching their hooves.

When it reached Wartle, he squealed and then grabbed his feet.

When it reached Jack, it sizzled, and smoke rose from his shoes.

Jack moved his hand away.

The queen marched toward him.

As she approached the Wicked Fairy, the queen began to change.

With each step, she was growing.

Taller, yes, but older too.

Now she looked eight.

Ten.

Twelve.

Fifteen.

Step by step, inch by inch, year by year.

Until finally, she wasn't a little girl at all. A proud and angry young woman reached Jack upon the dais. She looked into his pumpkin eyes, and she didn't have to look up to do it. She was as tall as he was. So she stared angrily at the Wicked Fairy. And he glared right back at the Good Fairy.

So, I bet you think he's going to get it now, don't you? Squash, pumpkin, squash!

"Well," said the queen, "what are you doing here?"

"Aren't you pleased to see Jack, dear?" he replied.

"You aren't supposed to be here, you know."

"Please forgive Jack. Let him kowtow."

The Wicked Fairy executed a mock bow.

"Stop rhyming everything I say."

"Jack can't help it. He's rhyming fey."

The queen sighed.

"Very well," she said. "Just tell me what is your business here, Jack."

"Ah," said the pumpkin.

"I bring you something that you lack.
I have it here inside my pack.
I'm sure you'll find it very sweet,
For now your crown can be complete."

Jack reached inside a worn and sorry-looking satchel. He lifted something out and offered it to the queen.

Curious gasped. It was a broken unicorn horn. A dozen new questions sprang to Curious's curious mind. But foremost among all the questions—where did Jack *get* the horn? Whose horn was it?

"He's gone too far," he whispered to Midnight. "This is it."

But the queen's eyes didn't grow angry. They lit up. She turned a smile on the Wicked Fairy that was nearly as wide as the one carved in his pumpkin shell.

"Oh, faithful Jack," she said. "Oh, glorious pumpkin! The last one!"

Queen Titania reached for the broken horn in Jack's hand.

But the Wicked Fairy stepped away.

And as he did so, a pumpkin vine that had been quietly questing about the queen's person withdrew with him.

"Winky," whispered Wartle. The puckle was right. The vine had plucked the Absorbing Orb containing the wispy wood wink from off the queen's royal person.

"Jack," said the queen sharply, "that's mine."

Jack held up a placating hand. Then the vine lifted its catch up to his face. Jack examined the wisp in the globe. In the presence of the Wicked Fairy, its blue light shone brightly. You could almost say it was a panicky blue light. Did it quiver just a little in the fairy's grasp? Maybe. Maybe not.

"This little wisp belongs with me,
Across the Restless River, see?
So give it here, you need not fear,
All you want so soon shall be."

Jack gestured at the crown with the unicorn horn.

The queen looked at it with greedy eyes. Then she snatched the horn from Jack's hand. The wisp and her orb were forgotten.

"It's beautiful," she said. "It practically ripples with magic. I can feel the power coursing through it."

Jack nodded, stepping back to give her space with the crown.

"Only the biggest horns I fetch,
And this one here was quite a catch.
A frightened filly who roamed too far.
Upon her brow she had a—"

"Quiet, Jack," said the queen, waving a hand to silence the pumpkin. "Don't spoil my mood with your inane rhymes. Not now, when all my plans are coming together."

She admired the horn a few more moments in her own palm, then slipped it into place in the front of the crown.

"Crown me, Jack," she said.

At her command, vines snaked out to lift the crown from its cushion. They gingerly settled it on Queen Titania's head.

"How do I look?"

Jack kissed his fingertips and winked.

The queen in her new crown truly was an impressive sight. Though it was a ghoulish sight too. Especially if you were a unicorn.

"His service done, Jack's off to fun.
I'll leave you now, your crown complete.
Until, fair queen, when next we meet."

Jack bowed deeply as he retreated. He would take a few steps, bow, a few more steps, a bow. Curious wasn't fooled. Neither was Midnight. It was an act. But they saw how the queen ate up the flattery. Watching her, Curious realized how pride blinded her. Glancing at Midnight, he saw how it had blinded him too.

When Jack disappeared through the mirror, the queen strode down the dais steps into the center of the room.

"Yes," she said with a smile. "I can feel the magic of the Crown of Horns. So much power. And so much to do. I only need to test it out. Perhaps"—and here her eyes drifted about the room—"on a wicked pair of misbehaving little horsies!"

The queen swished her fingers and Curious and Midnight found themselves carried on a puff of air.

But not Wartle. Wartle scurried aside at the last moment. He dashed through another tiny door. And like that, he was gone.

Meanwhile, Curious and Midnight sailed out from behind their hiding spot. It was like surfing on an invisible wave. It carried them straight to the queen. Then it deposited them in a frightened and embarrassed lump in the middle of the floor.

"*You're* not in my dungeon," she said to Midnight. "And *you're* not in the fairy ring in your glen," she said to Curious. "Neither one of you is where you are supposed to be, and *that* is a problem. It is a problem for me, true. But it's a bigger problem for you."

But Curious wasn't going to be discounted so easily.

"No, it isn't," Curious said. "I've got questions, and I *demand* answers. Why didn't you take Midnight home like you promised? What has Jack been doing? What is that *thing* on your head?"

Now, you would think that the queen would be angry at such an outburst. After all, a magical monarch isn't used to being yelled at. And nobody *demands* answers from a queen, fairy or otherwise.

But the queen just smiled. And maybe that was a little more frightening than if she had merely gotten angry.

"Let's take your questions in reverse order, shall we?" she said. "What is on my head? Why, it's my Crown of Horns. And it's very powerful. After all, it's full of all that unicorn healing magic. So let's just see what it can do."

And with that she pointed at Midnight.

"Come here, ugly horsey."

"Me?" said Midnight. She stepped away from the queen and whatever she was about to do.

"Why not you?" said the queen.

She tapped a finger to her forehead, right on the band of the crown.

A golden light, not unlike unicorn light but with a tinge of purple, began to shine from all the broken horns. Then a big beam of that light struck Midnight square in the forehead.

The night mare yelped. Fire and smoke arced from her hooves and mane and nose, but then she froze, transfixed. She was held in place by the beam of purple-tinged golden magic.

Midnight couldn't move. She couldn't flame. She couldn't snort. And she felt a pain right above her eyes where the purplish-golden light fell.

Then she felt something horrible.

Her wild fires were changing.

No, they were extinguishing! They were snuffing out!

Her fire was going! Her fire was gone!

Her wonderful midnight-black coloring was turning gray. Gray, and then silver. Midnight wasn't the color of midnight anymore.

And something was pushing hard at her skull. Something was sprouting. Right from her forehead, something was growing!

Curious gasped.

"What—what's happening to me?" Midnight stammered.

"You're . . . you're changing," he replied.

"Changing? Into what?"

But then she felt something pushing outward from her forehead. Jutting into the air. Curling around in a spiral. And she knew. Before Curious even spoke she knew.

"A unicorn," said Curious.

It was true.

Midnight was a unicorn.

A rather beautiful one. Silver-gray, with a blue-black mane and tail. And a large, gleaming golden horn.

"What have you . . . what have you done to me?" Midnight said.

"I've made you into a unicorn," said the fairy queen.

"What?" said Midnight. "That's impossible. I can't be a unicorn. I hate unicorns."

The queen shrugged.

"Well, now your life is complicated," she said. "But I've got things to do."

She moved her finger back and forth between the two horses, the two unicorns.

"Eena, mena, mona, mite," she said, reciting the old counting game.

Her finger settled on Midnight.

"Well, I guess that's fitting," said the fairy queen. She snapped her fingers, and Midnight became strangely calm.

"What?" said the queen, in response to Curious's look. "It's not like I'm going to walk to the Silent Stones. No, I'll go in style. On my own new mount."

She floated up onto Midnight's back. Then she tucked her fingers into Midnight's mane. They set off across the room. Heading for the mirror, which had begun to ripple again.

"Wait!" shouted Curious.

"No time to wait," said the queen.

"But . . . how can you have changed her into a unicorn?"

The fairy queen was already passing through the mirror. She looked over her shoulder at Curious.

"Oh, I didn't *change* her at all, you silly unicorn," said the queen. "Nothing so difficult. I just *healed* her."

"What do you mean, *'healed her'*?"

The queen disappeared through the mirror, taking Midnight with her.

Curious tried to follow, but he bumped his nose on the glass.

Behind him, he heard the distinct and very heavy sound of the doors to the room bolting shut.

He was alone. And he was trapped.

☙ 24 ❧

WARTLE GETS HIS OWN CHAPTER

The instant the queen's magic scooped up Midnight and Curious, Wartle had darted through a portal straight into Elsewhither, the bright and shining land from where all fairies came.

Elsewhither was much, much brighter than even the Glistening Isles. If you were there now, you'd have to squint your eyes and hope someone had invented sunglasses.

But Wartle didn't have to squint. This was his home. He capered along, scurrying through a gorgeous meadow full of giant flowers. Or maybe trees. Or maybe mushrooms. It was hard to get specific when in Elsewhither, because things didn't always stay what they were from one moment to the next like they do here.

It was also very hard to feel bad in Elsewhither, where everything was so beautiful and there was just so much magical energy everywhere. But Wartle was managing it.

He was worried about Curious. About Midnight. He was even worried about Winky.

But what could he do? Wartle the puckle. Who nobody regarded and nobody remembered.

The idea that a puckle could do anything against the might of a fairy queen was ridiculous. Preposterous. Absurd. Stupid-dupid.

But Curious was in trouble.

And when Curious was in trouble, the puckle knew what to do.

"Well," Wartle said, "looks like it's Wartle to the rescue again."

So he found another little fairy door, and back to the Glistening Isles he went.

He'd been walking in Elsewhither for a bit, so he didn't come out where he went in. He was still in the Court of Flowers, yes, but in another room.

A room full of the not-children. And lots of tables covered in tablecloths.

He scurried under a table and hid beneath the cloth.

Oh, but the smell from up above was really interesting.

He smelled cupcakes and flavored ice shavings and fruit and even occasional marshmallows. And it was all so, so, so tantalizingly close.

What was a puckle to do?

Wartle grabbed a corner of the tablecloth and tugged it a little bit. A little bit more. And a bit more again.

A tray of sugar biscuits tipped and fell.

Wartle shot out from the table and caught it before it clattered. Then he ducked into hiding again with his prize.

Oh, the sugar biscuits were good. He ate the entire tray of them, twenty in all, in half as many mouthfuls.

But what about his friend Curious?

Curious can get his own sugar biscuits.

No. What about the trouble Curious was in?

Oh, that.

Oh, right.

But first, one more snack from the table.

Wartle pulled another corner of the tablecloth.

And marshmallows rained down upon him.

He opened his mouth, and *gulp, gulp, gulp* they were gone.

It was time to rescue Curious.

Or . . . or he could dart under another table and see what treats it might offer first.

There was always time to rescue Curious later.

So scurry to another table he did. And tug and tug.

And *plop*—a tray of frosted cakes!

They didn't last long at all.

Neither did the creamed tarts.

Scamper and scurry to a third table.

Tug and tug.

But whatever was on this table was heavy. The table-cloth wasn't moving.

Wartle was not a puckle to be denied.

He slipped out from under cover, and he clambered up to the tabletop.

And there he saw a large silver platter full of—

"Fishy!" cried Wartle in delight.

There were plates of salmon, lots of salmon.

What Wartle didn't know was that these were all Salmon of Wisdom. But Wartle didn't care. He knew what he liked.

"Fishies!" he cried again.

Wartle began to stuff his face with scaly goodness. *Munch, munch, munch.* He was working his way through his third fish when he was spotted.

"Puckle!" shouted Baron Buttercup.

"Where?" said Wartle, looking back and forth before realizing who they meant.

"Eeeeeep!" screamed the Duchess of Daises. "Puckle, puckle, puckle!"

"Pleased to meet you," said Wartle, with a little bow.

"Kill it kill it KILL IT," shrieked Lady Lilac, flinging a marshmallow pie at Wartle.

"Gulp," said Wartle, swallowing the pie.

He gulped again as he saw a horde of not-children descending on him.

Wartle leapt to and fro on the table as little hands grasped for him. Platters of sweets were sent flying into the air, until the room was thick with sugar clouds.

It was high past time he left.

Wartle burped.

The burp didn't sound like a normal burp.

It came out hot and throaty, like a burp should. But there were words in it. Wise words.

"Honey is sweet, but don't lick it off a briar."

Wartle clamped his hands over his mouth.

The not-children were taken aback. Puckles weren't generally this eloquent.

"What did it say?" they said, pausing in their assault.

"Honey is sweet, but don't lick it off a briar," Wartle burped again.

"What does that mean?" asked the Duchess of Daisies.

"It means it's time to go," said Wartle. "Bye-bye."

He took the opportunity of their confusion to run for his life. He might really like fish and sweets, but he wasn't stupid.

CURIOUS COMES TO THE RESCUE.
HE REALLY DOES.

Curious was furious.

He was trapped in the Court of Flowers. A place no unicorn ever would have thought to be trapped.

And his friend Midnight—if she was his friend, if she was still Midnight—had been ridden away by the queen of the good fairies.

The good fairies who weren't that good.

He didn't know what the queen was up to exactly, but he knew he had to try to stop her if he could.

But more than that, he knew he had to help Midnight.

First, though, he had to get out of the room.

He ran to the door and gave it a shove. It wouldn't budge. Not an inch.

So then he spun around and gave it a good kick with both his back feet.

Bam. He made a loud noise, but that's all he made. Not even a dent. The wooden door held firm.

Bam. Curious kicked the door again.

"Hey," called a voice. "Cut that out. I can't hear myself think in here."

Curious looked around the room. He thought he was alone. He *was* alone.

He started to raise a hoof.

"I said knock it off," said the voice.

"Who are you?" said Curious. "Where are you? Are you invisible?"

"Invisible? Of course not," said the voice.

"Then are you very small?" asked Curious.

"I'm every bit as big as you are," said the voice. "Exactly as big. Or I will be, if you come closer."

That sounded almost like a puzzle. Curious was predictably curious.

The voice was definitely nearby. But he didn't see anyone. Then he thought about the words "I'll get bigger if you come closer."

If it were a puzzle, he had an idea how to solve it.

Curious trotted over to the mirror. He had heard about magic mirrors that could talk. And this mirror was certainly magical.

But he didn't see anything in the mirror. Just his own reflection. Of course, it got bigger as he got closer.

"There's no one here," said Curious.

"That's right," said his reflection. "There's no 'one' here. There's two here. Two of us."

"Oh my goodness," said Curious. "You're me."

The reflection blew an exasperated breath.

"Why do you automatically assume that I'm just a mirror version of you?"

"You are the one in the mirror. And you are my reflection."

"Not from where I'm standing," said the Mirror Curious.

Curious thought about this.

"Do you mean that you're looking in a magic mirror too?"

The Mirror Curious nodded.

"I know what you're thinking," he said. "You're thinking, if the Mirror Curious is looking in a magic mirror too, how do you even know you're the real Curious?"

"I am the real Curious," said Curious. But the reflection was right, he had been thinking that.

"I am the real Curious," mimicked the Mirror Curious.

"See? Who is to say you're not the reflection and the Curious you see in the mirror is the real one. How can you prove otherwise?"

He couldn't. Not yet.

But he was a unicorn with a Scientific Mind.

"I admit it's a bit of a puzzler," said Curious.

The Mirror Curious smiled. Or maybe it was the real Curious smiling. There had to be a way to figure this out.

"A real conundrum," said the reflection.

"It bears some thinking about," said Curious. He started to run through all the proofs of his own existence he could come up with.

"It's a good one," said the reflection. "Why, I imagine that a unicorn with a Scientific Mind could puzzle on this for hours."

"Days and days, even," agreed Curious. And then he stopped.

It was a good mystery. And he loved a good mystery.

So much so that he'd forgotten his friend was in trouble. He'd forgotten that the fairy queen was wearing a grisly crown made out of broken unicorn horns.

"This isn't a puzzle," said Curious. "It's a trap. The perfect trap for a curious unicorn. You're not the real me at all. You're just some shape-stealing fairy creature placed here by the queen to slow me down."

The reflected unicorn's face clouded with anger. Curious knew he had guessed correctly.

"Well," said the Mirror Curious, "it doesn't matter what I am. There's no way out of this room. You're still trapped."

He kicked angrily at a candle holder beside the mirror, and it fell over. Remarkably, the one on Curious's side of the mirror fell as well. This did not escape Curious's notice. He decided to experiment.

Ignoring his reflection, Curious kicked the remaining candle over too. But the one in the reflection didn't fall. It was still standing.

"It only works one way," said the Mirror Curious smugly. "I can affect things in your realm, but you have no power here."

Curious nodded. Although his reflection was being smug, Curious wasn't offended. He was gathering facts.

"No power here," said Curious. "I don't think you have it either."

"What are you talking about?" laughed the Mirror Curious. "I have so much power, I even took your shape."

"No," said Curious. "I think you're just as trapped as I am."

"I'm not trapped," said the Mirror Curious. "I'm *the* trap."

Curious shook his head.

"You're a distraction, that's all. The queen placed you in the trap with me so I wouldn't try to escape. That makes you every bit as much a prisoner here as I am."

"You're not right. You're wrong! Wrong!" said the Mirror Curious. But he was speaking a little bit too loud. "Unlike you, I can leave any time I like."

"Prove it," said Curious. "If you aren't trapped, go open that door." He gestured at the reflection of the big wooden doors in the glass.

The Mirror Curious took a few steps in that direction. But then he stopped.

"Wait," he said. "If I go open that door, it will open the one on your side. I'm not about to let you trick me like that so you can slip away."

"That's fine," said Curious. "Because that proves my point. You're trapped here too."

"I'm not!"

"I won't believe until I can see," said Curious. "We'll do it this way. I'll go stand way over there by the dais while you just open and shut the door. It's too far for me to get to the door in time. Then, when the door is closed, I'll come back and you can gloat about how wrong I was."

Curious could see the Mirror Curious was considering it.

"Otherwise, I'll just call you a liar," said Curious.

"Fine, we'll do it," said his reflection.

"Good," said Curious.

Curious repositioned the mirror. Then he trotted over to the dais. But when he turned around, his flank bumped the red-stained oak box, and it fell to the ground.

"Oops," he said. "Clumsy me." He noticed that the reflection of the oak box in the mirror hadn't fallen. Just as he had expected.

"Let's just get this over with," called his reflection.

"Ready when you are," said Curious.

The Mirror Curious stretched out a hoof, and pushed one of the two heavy wooden doors. It swung open easily. So did one of the two wooden doors on Curious's side of the mirror.

"There, you see," said Mirror Curious. "I'm not trapped."

"You're not," said Curious. "And now, neither am I."

Curious gave the oak box a shove. It slid across the smoothly polished floor.

Mirror Curious withdrew his hoof, and the door started to close slowly. But on Curious's side of the mirror, the oak box slid into the door as it swung shut, trapping it open.

"No!" the Mirror Curious shrieked. His door was closed, but Curious's was open. The reflection looked in panic to where the reflection of the oak box still rested upon its cushion on the dais.

"It only works one way," Curious reminded him.

The Mirror Curious charged across his room, heading for the oak box. If he could smash it or move it or something, he could affect the one on Curious's side.

But Curious was running for the door.

It was a race—Curious against Curious.

Fortunately, our Curious reached the door just as Mirror Curious brought a hoof down, smashing the oak box to splinters.

The real oak box exploded too.

Too late.

Curious stretched out a leg and caught the door before it swung shut.

"I'll get you for this! I'll get you!" screeched the Mirror Curious.

"I don't think so," said Curious. "I'm not trapped anymore. But I'm pretty sure when the queen returns and finds me gone, you will be."

The Mirror Curious's expression went from anger to fear, and he looked around his reflected room in a panic.

"Help me," he said.

"I'll wish you good luck," said Curious. "But I'm not staying." And he trotted out the door.

He was free.

But although he was free, Curious still had a problem.

Queen Titania had ridden Midnight through the mirror. He couldn't follow. To get to the Silent Stones, he'd have to go the long way, across the River Restless.

He thought about how to accomplish this as he made his way through the twisting, honey-colored corridors of the Court of Flowers.

That's when he bumped into Wartle.

"May the roof above you never fall in and those gathered beneath it never fall out," said Wartle with a burp.

"What?" said Curious in surprise.

"I said, 'Hello,'" said Wartle.

"I'm pretty sure you didn't. But it's good to see you. Climb on, we're in a hurry."

Wartle swung up onto Curious's back. Then together they raced from the Court of Flowers. Soon they were back in the Willowood and running as fast as Curious could run.

"Where are we going?" said Wartle.

"We're looking for Poor Mad Tom," Curious explained. "He's got to take us across the river and fast."

There was, unfortunately, a problem with that plan. When they found Tom, they saw it for themselves.

Poor Tom's poor raft had been shattered into about two dozen separate planks when it was roughly cast upon the shore by the Swan Boat's wave. The boy was busy with a hammer and nails rebuilding it. But he had a lot of work still to do.

"She's not keeping us afloat as she is," he explained as Curious stared at the wreckage. "Poor Tom is sorry, for you and him, because Tom needs to return to the safety of the river. Though the fairy won't mess with Tom as long as he has plenty of these about."

He held up a long iron nail, then set to hammering it into a plank.

Curious remembered how the fairy queen wouldn't step on Tom's raft.

"Tom," he said, "Queen Titania fussed at you for using nails in your raft. Why did she do that?"

Poor Mad Tom grinned.

"The Fair Folk can't abide the touch of iron," he said. "It burns their otherworldly flesh like fire and ice together."

"Iron," said Curious. He recalled how Jack had recoiled from the two horses when they had sheltered under the covered bridge.

"The horseshoe. It was made of iron too."

"Aye, it was. Tom caught it when you dropped it. A handy thing it is." The boy fished in his pocket and withdrew the horseshoe.

Curious had an idea.

No, he had a Plan. Like one of Midnight's Plans.

He'd have to test it to see if it worked. So it was both a Plan and an Experiment.

"Tom," he said, "I want you to shoe my hoof with that horseshoe."

Wartle gasped. And Tom looked shocked.

"It would be a blasphemy to shoe such a wild and noble creature as a unicorn."

Curious didn't know much about the world of people that Tom came from, but he knew that horses there had hard lives serving as mounts for their masters.

"Maybe it is a blasphemy," he said, "but I don't care. A Scientific Mind isn't afraid of anything when in pursuit of a noble goal. I need that horseshoe."

Wartle offered his hands helpfully. But Curious shook his head.

"Thank you, Wartle, but I need to be able to use it myself. I can't risk you dropping it or having it taken away."

He lifted his front right hoof and offered it to Tom.

The boy hesitated.

"Are you sure?" he asked.

"Just do it," said Curious.

So Poor Mad Tom took his hammer and his nails and the horseshoe made of iron. And he set to work.

⚘ **26** ⚘

CROSSING THE RIVER RESTLESS

"Aren't you that unicorn we tried to drown?"

"That would be me."

Curious stood on the banks of the River Restless. He had a nervous puckle clutching the hairs of his mane and an unfamiliar piece of iron nailed to his hoof.

He had run upriver, away from Tom's raft and closer to the point where he first met Midnight. Having the horseshoe on his foot felt strange. It felt even stranger having shod one foot only. It made his forelegs feel slightly uneven.

Ahead of him, the kelpies were floating in a loose line. Curious saw the water dripping from the icky green seaweed of their manes. They grinned wickedly and gnashed their nasty yellow teeth in anticipation of a good unicorn drowning. *Gnash, gnash, gnash,* their teeth went.

"Well, we're going to drown you for real this time if you set one hoof in the river," said the kelpie who had spoken before.

"One hoof," said Curious. "Just one? You mean, like this?"

He trotted forward and stuck his right hoof into the rushing water.

Several kelpies lunged at him, and he bolted back.

"What was that for?" asked Wartle.

"I was testing the range of the horseshoe," said Curious. "They weren't affected by my dipping it in the water. Now I need to see what direct kelpie contact does." He smiled to give himself courage. "Are you ready to conduct our Experiment?"

"You'll never plow a field by turning it over in your mind," burped Wartle.

"Wartle," said Curious. "I couldn't have put that better myself."

"Neither could I," said Wartle.

Curious leapt into the water.

Splash.

Wartle screamed, and the kelpies all neighed in delight. They converged on the unicorn. This was going to be fun, they thought.

But they were very wrong.

Curious kicked out at them with his right foot.

Unfortunately, he wasn't much of a fighter and his kicks didn't have anything like the force that Midnight put into hers.

Fortunately, he didn't need to be a fighter. The first kelpie his shoed-hoof brushed against hollered in pain. The kelpie swam away, a horseshoe-shaped burn mark seared into its scales. A smell of charred seafood wafted over the river.

Curious kicked again and another kelpie hollered. "Ow, ow, ouch!"

Then something grabbed Curious by the tail and dragged him under.

Down, down, down he went toward the bottom of the river.

Kelpies struck and bit at him all around.

Wartle clung desperately to his mane.

Curious twisted this way and that, dishing out burning horseshoe brands to kelpie after kelpie. They didn't like it. Not one bit.

So they retreated.

Curious swam with all four legs, pumping as hard as he could.

He broke the surface of the water, sucking air into his lungs.

He had escaped drowning for a second time.

"The greater the hurry, the more obstacles there are," burped Wartle as Curious climbed out on the southern shore.

"Then we better get on with it," said Curious.

They charged into the Whisperwood.

Which was every bit as dark and nasty and foreboding as it had been the last time.

"Do you know where we are?" Curious asked Wartle.

"A word to the wise, a stick to the unwise," the puckle replied.

Wartle clamped his little hands over his mouth.

He pointed to the barest, faintest, thinnest suggestion of a path.

It was hard to see. Very hard to see.

But Curious's horn started glowing. A soft golden light.

It wasn't much, but in the darkness of the Whisperwood it was enough.

So Curious and Wartle made their winding way through the forest.

And they almost got to the Silent Stones without incident.

Almost.

Because right when they thought they were going to have an uneventful trip through the most dangerous forest ever, a pair of very long, eerily thin, and disgustingly slimy tendrils plopped down and draped themselves all over Wartle and a good portion of Curious's neck.

It was like having spaghetti noodles dumped all over you, though neither Wartle nor Curious had ever seen spaghetti. So to them it was just very slimy and gross.

"Ew! Gross!" said Curious.

"Ew! Slimy!" said Wartle.

The noodle things wrapped Wartle up and lifted him into the air. He struggled like a puppet with its strings in a twist.

Curious leapt after his friend.

And a pair of nasty teeth snapped at him.

Two pairs.

In two very nasty heads.

The heads looked like the heads of wild-eyed and very dirty humans, but with wispy gray cobwebs for hair, and sharp and pointed teeth.

And they had no bodies. At least, no bodies apart from the slimy noodle things that descended from where their necks should be. The long, ropey bits looked a little like snakes, a little like worms, and a little like intestines.

Curious thought that there were two of the creatures, but their noodly bodies were all tangled together. Which is how the creatures got their name.

"Tangleheads!" cried Wartle, in full-on puckle panic. He was panicking because he'd seen Tangleheads before. He knew their favorite food was puckle!

Curious bit at the slimy threads snaring his friend. They made him want to gag, but still he bit and tugged.

But Tangleheads are nothing if not tenacious. They started wrapping Curious up too. Soon he was hoisted into the air alongside Wartle.

"What do we do?" yelled Curious.

Wartle felt a big belch of platitudes forming in his belly, but he shoved it down and forced his mouth to obey.

"Untangle! Untangle!" he yelped.

Curious didn't understand.

Of course, they wanted to get untangled. They were both covered in the nasty noodles.

He pulled a noodle with his teeth.

"No!" screamed Wartle. "Untangle *them*!"

"I'm trying to!" shouted Curious.

"From each other!"

Oh. Curious began to pull the threads apart.

It was hard, because they kept twisting. But Curious realized he still had his horseshoe. He pressed his foot on different bits of ropey body, chasing it away, and then he started pulling the bits apart.

It took work, but it did *work.*

Finally the two Tanglehead bodies separated. And when they did, all the noodles let go.

Curious and Wartle fell.

The tendrils recoiled into the heads like the snapping-back tongues of two toads.

Two heads dropped to the ground.

The heads hissed angrily at the unicorn and the puckle.

Then they rolled away like bowling balls and disappeared into the woods.

"We did it," said Curious.

"Lose an hour in the morning, and you'll be looking for it all day," burped Wartle.

"You're right," said Curious. "No time to waste."

And on through the woods they ran.

Before long, they came to the cave of the Slumbering Cindersloth. But as far as Curious could tell, it was still slumbering.

He knew the way from there, but he had no idea how to rescue Midnight, nor what exactly he was rescuing her from.

Curious saw a light through the trees. He heard noises echoing through the woods.

The light was a golden-light. Nearly a unicorn light.

And the noise, the noise was of a hundred tiny feet.

Suddenly, a half a hundred Wicked Fairy Creatures burst from the woods.

There were bolkers and coblins, dwirts and frownies, glaistigs and gomboblins! They were running straight for Curious and Wartle.

But the Fairy Creatures weren't coming for them.

They were fleeing!

"Look out!" cried Curious. "It's a stampede!"

Gwrols, hobthrusts, and kolatoons came pouring from the trees! Nurts, pigganders, and salpucks came bursting from the undergrowth! Spriders, trolicaun, and uckies came leaping from the branches!

They flapped and slithered and crawled and swarmed all around Curious and Wartle. The unicorn and the puckle were jostled and scratched, bumped and jumped. But none of the Wicked Fairy Creatures paid them any attention. They were too busy fleeing. And then, as swiftly as they had appeared, they were gone.

Wartle swayed on his little legs.

"I don't feel so good," he said.

He started to fall. But he caught Curious's horn. The horn's golden glow pulsed with light. Wartle steadied.

"Better," said the puckle.

Interesting, thought Curious. Something was making Wartle feel sick. And something was making the Wicked Fairies flee. He hurried on, anxious to find his friend, eager to know the reason.

CURIOUS ABOUT MIDNIGHT

Now, I imagine you are wondering what Queen Titania has been up to since she dove into the magic mirror. And I certainly hope you are wondering what has happened to our friend Midnight now that she has been transformed into a unicorn.

Well, if you are, you aren't alone. Because Midnight has been wondering the exact same things.

Midnight wondered if she just *looked* like a unicorn, or was she a unicorn, you know, *on the inside*?

Would she have to leave the Curse and go live in the Wil-lowood? Was she expected to be empty-headed and giddy now? Was she supposed to prance and dance and chase butterflies and fart rainbows? Could she fart rainbows?

Was that something you did on purpose or did it just *happen*?

Jumping through the magic mirror only took a moment. The portal spat them out into the Whisperwood, very near the Hidden Glen. Assuming they hadn't left the Silent Stones now that she'd *broken* them, she'd see the Curse very soon. That was really something to wonder about.

The Curse were already mad at her. What would they think now that she wasn't a night mare anymore?

She wasn't a night mare anymore. Oh, that was hard to grasp.

What would the Curse do about that?

Well, she was about to find out.

Because the fairy monarch rode Midnight right into the Hidden Glen.

Midnight's clean coat was all shiny. Her new horn was all glowy. Her new mane all golden and lushy. Titania was all bright colors and youthful, flowing locks and gleaming crown. Together, they looked like they'd climbed right out of a masterful painting or a thrilling storybook.

The night mares all leapt into the air, they were so

shocked. They neighed and snorted in fear. Old Sooty was so alarmed that she farted a burst of black smoke that propelled her ten feet through the air.

Only one night mare in all the Curse kept it together. Can you guess who? Only the biggest, strongest, fiercest night mare in the entire herd. It was Sabledusk, of course. Who else would it be?

"Queen Titania," said Sabledusk, trotting up to them and looking for all the world as if she had everything under control or soon would. "We did not expect this visit. What are you doing in our Whisperwood? You are a long way from the Court of Flowers."

The queen looked down on Sabledusk from where she rode on Midnight's back. Her upper lip curled in a sneer.

"Silly pony," said the queen. "Speaking as if we were equals. If you know what's good for you, you'll take your Curse and gallop out of here as fast as your flaming hooves can carry you. Or I'll show you a Curse, oh, I will."

Well, you can imagine how that went over with Sabledusk. But in case you can't, I'll tell you.

Not. Very. Well.

Sabledusk's eyes positively glowed with anger and her mane burst into bright yellow flame. She reared up on her back legs and she shouted, "Someone is leaving here as fast as their hooves can go, but it isn't the Curse!"

Midnight actually shied back a step. It was her own hooves, after all, that Sabledusk was talking about. Her mother hadn't recognized her. She wanted to say something, to let Sabledusk know it was her. But she hesitated. Sabledusk had never looked as fierce or as strong before. She was proud of her mother, but also a little afraid of her too.

Queen Titania merely laughed at the burning, blazing black horse that towered before her.

"Out of my way, you ugly, ugly creature," she said, and she raised a hand. Her fingers started twitching, and Midnight guessed very accurately that the queen was about to cast a spell. With that worry, she found her voice.

"Wait! That's my mother!"

Sabledusk snorted in surprise.

Then Titania laughed a mean little chuckle.

"Night mare," said the queen, "my mount seems to think she's your daughter. Is this true?"

Sabledusk's flames rose a full foot into the air before she spoke.

"Don't be ridiculous, fairy," she said. Midnight could hear the disgust in her voice. "That's a *unicorn.* No unicorn would ever be a daughter of mine."

"Mom . . . ," Midnight said in a soft voice. But no one heard her now.

Queen Titania completed her spell.

A ray of golden-y, purply light zipped from the queen's fingers. The night mares were all picked up and cast away in the force of the blast, flung into the Whisperwood.

"Mom!" yelled Midnight. She caught Sabledusk's eye as her mother was hurled away. But it was too late. Because now the queen placed her fingertips to either side of the band of the Crown of Horns, right above her temples. She closed her eyes, concentrating.

For a moment, nothing happened.

And then the Crown of Horns let loose.

❦ 28 ❦

SILENT NO MORE

There was a great big golden light shining from the Crown of Horns. It arced up into the air like water from a fountain. It fell down upon the center stone like rain from the sky.

And the center stone seemed to suck it up, to drink it in, to gulp it down like a thirsty beast. All that golden light pouring into the parched rock.

Then, to Midnight's surprise, the center stone began to stir, lifting itself inch by inch until it was standing straight up again.

And then it moved. It shuffled back and forth, dragging

its weight across the ground, until it was exactly where it used to be. Good as new.

As new? Not yet.

Because then the golden light poured from the center stone, flowing like a wave of honey, until it engulfed all the other stones.

Those stones that had tipped or toppled over across the many, many centuries straightened up too. Soon all the stones looked like they were standing at attention. Like they were awake and alert and ready for anything. Now they were good as new.

Nope.

The moss and the dirt that had covered them for centuries suddenly dried up, flaked off, and blew away in a cloud of greenish-grayish dust.

Then all the long-faded runes carved into the stones, the runes that had been worn down and become hard to read anymore, became very clear and very visible. The runes began to glow in reddish-goldish light.

Now the stones truly were as good as new.

Midnight realized then what the queen was doing. She wasn't *changing* the stones. She was *healing* the Silent Stones. She was using the healing power of all those stolen unicorn horns to repair the Silent Stones and make them what they used to be when they were first made. Now they were exactly what they had been when long-forgotten druids had placed them here to protect the islands from the fairy folk.

And Midnight had a thought. Had she really been changed? Or had she been—

But then her thoughts were interrupted. Because the Silent Stones were silent no longer. No, the Silent Stones began to sing.

It was like a humming at first. Then it was like a chanting. It swelled in volume. It grew until it was like the sound of boulders tumbling down a mountain. Like the rumbling sound of rocks shifting below the earth. Now they were the Singing Stones.

Midnight heard hollering and complaining, yelping, barking, whining. She heard mewing, cawing, and squawking. Because every Wicked Fairy and Wicked Fairy Creature lurking in the woods beyond the Hidden Glen was suddenly very, very uncomfortable. After all, they had never liked the Silent Stones very much to begin with, even when they had lost most of their power and were just old, moss-covered rocks. They certainly didn't like the Singing Stones when they were actually singing and doing it at full blast. So they were hollering. And they were fleeing. Midnight heard the sound of their many feet and wings and scales as they ran and flew and slithered away.

Then Midnight heard something else. Hoofbeats. Approaching.

Someone was coming here when everyone else was leaving.

Curious galloped into the Hidden Glen.

"Midnight!" he shouted.

She was astounded. Her friend had come for her again.

Midnight tried to move closer to Curious. But the queen gave her mane a tug and held the night mare in place. Something about the fairy queen's grip sent shivers all down her neck and into her forelegs, and they refused to obey any orders but Titania's. She was stuck. But Curious saw, and he understood.

"Don't worry," he said. "I'm here to rescue you."

"*You* rescue *me*?"

"It's sort of my turn, isn't it?" he said. Then Curious looked at the Singing Stones, and he listened to their wordless song, and Midnight could almost see his Scientific Mind putting it all together.

"I know what she's doing," Curious said.

"What?"

"By restoring the stones," he explained, "she's driving away all the Wicked Fairies."

"But won't she be affected too?"

"Not while she wears the crown."

"True," agreed Wartle, still clinging to Curious's horn.

"What about her own court? And all the good fairies in her part of the isle? Won't they be driven out too?"

The queen spoke up.

"I'll stop the stones' singing before that happens. Once all the Wicked Fairies are gone, I'll destroy the stones. The entire isle will be mine!"

"Well, that does sound like a good plan," admitted Curious.

"Curious!" Midnight was aghast.

"I don't mean 'good' as in 'good,'" he explained. "I mean 'good' as in it would work."

"It *is* working," said the queen. She looked down at Midnight, on whose back she still rode. "You're a unicorn now. If we get rid of all the Wicked Fairies, you and your new friends can have the whole island."

Midnight didn't know what to say. The Curse slept inside the circle of the Silent Stones for *protection* from Wicked Fairy Creatures at night. So if they were gone, the woods would be a lot nicer. Then, she supposed, unicorns *could* have the whole island. And she *was* a unicorn. She didn't belong in the Curse. The Curse . . .

"But what about the night mares?" she asked.

"What about them?" asked the queen. "I suppose I'll have to deal with them separately at some point."

"Deal with them?" said Curious.

"Well, once I've converted all this dreary woods into something prettier, I can't have ugly burning horses running about. They'd scorch my flowers."

"But my mother . . ."

"Didn't recognize you," said the queen. "And wouldn't want you as you are anyway. And really, why would you want *her*? We can find you a much better mommy if you need one. One who is charming and sweet and never fusses at you for misbehaving. And now you'll be a much better daughter than you ever were before. And everyone will like you."

A better daughter. Midnight had always wanted to be a better daughter. But not by being a unicorn. Not because she'd been turned into someone else. She wanted to control her fire. Now she didn't have to worry about controlling her fire anymore because she didn't have any. She'd have new magics, unicorn magics. And . . . she wanted to be liked.

It was tempting. All she had to do was . . . nothing. She could just sit back and let the queen drive away every bit of her old life and give her a new one.

She looked at the only other unicorn in the glen. The one who had come to rescue her. He had come to rescue her before, too, when she was still a night mare. Night mare or unicorn, he didn't care.

That settled it.

"Curious," said Midnight. "I can't do anything with the queen on my back. Do you know how to get this mangy monarch off me?"

"He wouldn't dare," said the queen. "And anyway, he wouldn't know how."

Curious bobbed his head.

"Don't be so sure, Your Majesty. In fact, I have an Experiment in progress. You'll like it, Midnight," he added. "It's like one of your Plans."

Curious charged at the queen. She saw him coming and pointed a finger his way. A bolt of purple light zapped toward him. But he raised his iron-shod hoof and the light split in two, zipping away to either side.

The queen gasped.

Curious reared up and touched the queen with his horseshoe.

"It burns! It burns! It burns!" she screamed. She tumbled from Midnight's back.

Midnight leapt clear of her.

"What is that thing doing on your hoof?" she asked.

"It's an iron horseshoe," said Curious. "Turns out fairies can't stand iron," he explained to Midnight.

Titania glowered at Curious.

"We can't," she said. "But iron or no iron, I'll deal with you in a moment. Right after I've finished this."

The air behind her twitched. Gossamer wings grew

from her shoulders. Queen Titania rose above the ground. Curious leapt for her, but she was too high.

Honey light flowed from the crown, and the transformation of the stones continued. Curious and Midnight couldn't reach her, so they couldn't stop her.

"There's nothing we can do," cried Midnight.

Things were bad. They were so bad, our heroes didn't see how they could get any worse.

But you know that's not true.

No matter how bad things are . . .

Things can *always* get worse.

Because just at that moment, who should come riding into the clearing but that bothersome fairy, Jack o' the Hunt?

✧ 29 ✧

THINGS GET WORSE THAN WORSE

Jack o' the Hunt rode upon the poor, unfortunate new night mare.

> "A wondrous plan, one must confess
> But not, Jack thinks, the very best.
> For while she plotted, toiled, and dreamed,
> Jack labored toward another scheme."

Another scheme? thought Curious.

"Jack," he asked. "What are you doing here?"

"How is he *here* at all?" asked Midnight. "He's a fairy. Shouldn't the Singing Stones drive him away?"

The pumpkin head beamed at Midnight.

"If Jack sets foot upon the ground,
He'd have to scream and turn around.
But Jack is safe by all account,
When seated on a night mare mount.
But no time has Jack to treat with you,
For Pumpkin Jack has things to do.
The stones a-singing will not stop,
So to another world they'll drop."

Well, that made Curious's ears perk up. *Another world?* He didn't have long to wonder, though. Because next Jack motioned with his tattered gloves, and from out of the Whisperwood floated a pumpkin shell. Inside the pumpkin was the Absorbing Orb, and in the Orb . . .

"Winky!" cried Wartle. He reached with both hands toward the pumpkin. Instantly all the singing from the stones made him woozy, so he quickly clamped his fingers back on Curious's horn.

"Ahhhhhhhhh," said Wartle with a long sigh.

Wartle was right, though. It was Winky in the pump-kin, lighting it up with bluish light. And following behind this floating vegetable lantern came none other than Sable-dusk.

"Mom!"

But Sabledusk didn't respond. She didn't take her gaze off the pumpkin bobbing in the air before her. Sabledusk had a dreamy, faraway look in her eyes.

"She's *charmed*!" Midnight yelled to Curious. "Just like you were."

She wasn't the only one.

Another pumpkin and another floated out of the woods. And more mesmerized mares trotted along behind them.

There was Midnight's friend Vision. There was Dark-cloud, and Phantasm, and Shadowbutt. Every member of the Curse. Even Old Sooty.

They were all charmed. All mesmerized by a line of floating winks-in-orbs-in-pumpkins, and Jack was leading them.

"Now round and round we all must go,
And when we stop, Jack only knows!"

Jack led the Curse in a ring around the stones. He drove his heels into the new night mare's flanks, and she broke into a gallop. All the night mares galloped.

"Stop!" cried Midnight. "Stop!"

But they didn't stop. They only sped up.

The fairy queen concentrated on pouring out golden light. Maybe her magic would be more powerful than whatever Jack was doing. Or maybe not.

Faster and faster around the ring the pumpkins spun and the night mares ran. The air grew purple. The singing of the stones began to fade, as though it was coming from far away. One by one, the stones began to sink into the ground.

Only it wasn't ground. It was a big, gaping, smoking vortex where the ground used to be. Through the hole, Curious and Midnight could see the shimmering, shifting shapes of some other place.

Floating in the air, the fairy queen gritted her teeth under the strain. She was pouring all the healing magic she could into the stones, but it wasn't enough. They were slipping away. And Jack was singing again.

"Night mares, when they run at speeds,
Have powers beyond normal steeds
To open doors to other lands,
So Jack feeds on night mares when he can.
But now Jack runs them in a ring
To rid us of the stones that sing

And when the stones have gone away,
All Jack's friends will come to play."

"Jack's opening up a portal, like the mirror," said Curious. "That's what he meant by dropping them into another world. He's getting rid of the Singing Stones."

"But the Singing Stones keep the Wicked Fairies away," said Midnight. "Even the Silent Stones did that."

"Exactly," said Curious. "If we can't stop him, there'll be nothing keeping even the biggest, baddest Wicked Fairies from coming from Elsewhither. The Glistening Isles will be overrun with the most powerful Wicked Fairies."

Midnight ran after Sabledusk.

"Mother, stop! You've got to stop! Snap out of it!"

But Sabledusk didn't stop. She didn't reply at all. Not even when Midnight shoved her.

"I can't stop them," said Midnight.

And she was right.

And that was bee-ay-dee *bad.*

Because if you thought the Whisperwood had some nasty things in it before, what was coming soon would be a thousand times worse.

Midnight and Curious could see some of them. Vile and nasty creatures that were appearing in the shadows of the trees. And some things that were taller than the trees.

Things that were so big they could never have come to the Glistening Isles before.

Boobries and black dogs, salpucks and dwirts, sluagh and nuckelavees. And I am sorry to tell you this, but there's not much that is nastier than a nuckelavee.

The fairy queen saw all these Wicked Fairies too. She twisted in the air, fighting to pour more and more healing power into the stones. But it still wasn't enough.

"Oh, what do we do? What do we do?" said Midnight.

"I don't know," said Curious.

Curious looked at the night mares. He saw their yellow fires. He saw the purple light of the portal they were opening. He saw the reddish-golden light of the glowing runes of the Singing Stones.

These were all the colors of magic. He might not fart rainbows, but he knew what rainbows were. All the colors were just different shades of the same light. And all the colors of magic, they were different shades too. Right now the purple magic was winning. They needed magic of another color. Magic of a goldish, reddish variety. And lots of it. Like Midnight's wild fire. That was powerful magic.

He remembered how it had charged the Silent Stones when it was under control. How it had blown the center stone over when she'd lost that control.

"Midnight," he said. "I don't think your wild fire hurt the Silent Stones. I think it overpowered them."

"What are you saying?" asked Midnight.

"They could use some of that extra power now to drown out Jack's magic."

"But I don't have my fire anymore," she said. "I'm a unicorn now."

"I know," Curious said. "But what we need is fire. I wish you were still a night mare."

"You do?" said Midnight. "If I were a night mare, then we couldn't be friends."

"Of course we'd be friends," said Curious. "We'll always be friends."

Midnight thought about that. And what she wanted to be. Who she really was. In all her wild, untamed, fiery self.

"My wild fire would really help now?" she asked.

"Yes," said Curious. "Forgive me, but I wish the fairy queen hadn't changed you into a unicorn."

"Oh, but she didn't," said Midnight. "She didn't *change* me at all."

"What are you talking about?"

"She didn't *change* me," said Midnight. "She *healed* me. I—and all of us night mares—we are unicorns. We've *always* been unicorns."

"I don't understand," said Curious.

"Then I'll show you."

Then Midnight lifted her head high.

And brought it down hard.

She smashed her horn on the ground.

And it broke right off.

Wild fire poured from her forehead.

Wild fire shot from her hooves.

Wild fire danced from her mane.

And in the heat of that wild fire, she changed back to her old self again. And she was blazing. And beautiful.

And maybe because she was the one in charge now, she didn't lose her memories or forget where she was or who she was. She was Midnight, the night mare, and she was going to save the day.

"Now stand back," she said. "I can't control this. *And I'm not gonna try.*"

"What are you going to do?" asked Curious.

"I'm going to Stomp!"

And Stomp she did.

Midnight stomped circles around the Curse. She stomped circles around Jack o' the Hunt. She danced in and she danced out. She stomped her feet as hard as she'd ever stomped. And her fire was as wild as ever. As wild as it was on the day she first lost her horn. And any wild day thereafter.

Where she stomped, her fire leapt through the ring of running night mares. And it struck the Singing Stones. Now they blazed in reddish-golden light.

It was so bright and blazing, in fact, that Sabledusk had

trouble seeing the wispy wood wink in its pumpkin shell. And so did Vision and Stormcloud, and Phantasm, and Shadowbutt, and Old Sooty. In fact, all the night mares were finding that the blazing light of Midnight's wild fire was filling up their eyes and awakening them from being charmed. As they woke, they slowed down. Their own fires began to flicker in time with Midnight's. In fact, all the fires burned the same color.

"No, no, no!" shouted Jack.
"That's not the way this is supposed to go.
You're all my ponies, it's very true. . . ."

"You know what," said Curious. "I'm sick of you."
He leapt and kicked Jack in his pumpkin head with his ironshod foot. Jack hollered as the horseshoe burnt his shell. And he kept hollering as the pumpkin flew right off Jack's body and crashed into the Whisperwood.

Jack's headless body leapt from the back of the new night mare and chased after the head, crashing into the forest. They heard it crashing through the undergrowth, and then it was gone.

But then Midnight's fire reached critical level.
It *exploded.*
Kaboom!

⚜ 30 ⚜

THINGS GET BETTER . . . FOR NOW

Midnight stood alone in the center of a big ring of burned grass. Smoke rose from the ground. Her ears were ringing.

Atop her head, she wore the Crown of Horns. It must have fallen there, in the aftermath of the explosion.

"Wh-what happened?" she said.

"You did it," said Curious.

He trotted over to her, careful where he put his hooves. Little fires blazed everywhere.

"The stones?" she asked.

"See for yourself."

Around them, the Silent Stones were back where they had always been. Or mostly. One or two of them might have switched places.

"They aren't singing anymore," said Midnight.

"No," said Curious. "I think they are pretty worn out."

"Sleepy," said Wartle from Curious's back.

Wartle hopped to the ground and began to sniff around.

It wasn't long before he discovered what he was looking for.

"Winky!" he shouted. Wartle lifted an Absorbing Orb out of the remains of a smashed and smoldering pumpkin shell.

The various members of the Curse were shaking their manes and stamping their feet. They looked like they'd all woken up from a dream. Or maybe, if you'll pardon me, a nightmare.

Each horse had a burnt and smoldering pumpkin shell in front of it.

"What do we do now?" said Curious.

"We should let the wisps go free," said Midnight.

"All of them?" said Curious. "You don't want one to focus your fire?"

"I like my fire as it is," said Midnight. "Unfocused and wild. But what about you? Don't you need to study the colors of magic?"

"I think I've collected enough data for now," said

Curious. "Though of course I'm still interested in the subject."

Midnight nodded.

Then she stamped on an Absorbing Orb. It shattered, and a wispy wood wink flew into the air.

Following her lead, the horses of the Curse all stamped the orbs in front of them.

Soon the air was alive with glowing blue lights. But they weren't mesmerizing this time. Maybe they knew who had rescued them.

The wispy wood winks bobbed away into the forest.

"Good-bye, Winky," said Wartle sadly.

But then the last one turned. It floated back and began to circle the puckle.

"Winky!" Wartle cried in delight. He ran around in happy circles. The wisp seemed happy too.

"Is that everything, then?" asked Curious.

"No, it's not everything," snarled the fairy in their midst.

"Who are *you*?" asked Curious.

The little fairy was thin and mousy, somewhat frumpy and disheveled. She had whiskers and long, droopy ears. And she was covered with the goopy, smoldering insides of burst and burnt pumpkin.

But the look in her eyes was unmistakable.

"Titania?" asked Midnight.

"You're supposed to say 'Your Majesty,'" the fairy replied.

"What happened to *you*?"

"*You* happened to me, you stupid pony."

"I think she burned herself out," explained Curious. "All that power coursing through her burned up her glamour. This is the real Titania, when she isn't spinning illusions."

The queen glared at Curious angrily. Then she pointed at the Crown of Horns on Midnight's head.

"Well," she said, "what are you waiting for?"

"What am *I* waiting for?" asked the night mare.

"You won. You have the crown now. Use it."

"Use it for what?"

The fairy snorted.

"To turn yourself into a unicorn again," she said. "And to heal the Silent Stones."

"Lady," said Curious, "we just stopped you from doing that. Why would we do it now?"

"Because then you can drive out all the Wicked Fairies from the Whisperwood," said Titania. "You can all be unicorns. You can have the entire isle to yourselves. Everything can be beautiful."

"I don't think so," said Midnight. "I don't think everything that is beautiful *is* beautiful. Not really. And I think a lot of things that aren't beautiful really *are*."

"That doesn't make any sense," said the queen.

"I think it does," said Midnight. "Anyway, I'm not ready to judge who's really a Good Fairy and who's a Wicked one. I don't think anyone should do that. Certainly not *you*."

"You simpleminded, ugly little pony," said the queen. "Give me that."

She made a grab for the Crown. But she was tiny now, and weak.

"Don't you understand?" she said. Titania cast her eyes around at the Curse. "You could all be unicorns. All of you."

She tried to take the crown again.

Just then something really big lumbered out of the Whisperwood. It was furry and sleepy. It had little red worms of flame running all over it.

"It's the Slumbering Cindersloth!" roared Old Sooty.

The Slumbering Cindersloth raised its nose in the air, and it gave a great *SNIFF.*

SNIFF, SNIFF, SNIFF, it went.

It brought its nose to bear right in front of Queen Titania.

"There's something you should know," said Midnight to the monarch. "The Slumbering Cindersloth *really* likes pumpkin."

The queen looked at the giant Cindersloth. Then she looked at the pumpkin innards spattered all over her.

"Oh," she said.

"You really might want to run now," suggested Midnight.

The queen ran.

With a happy bellow, the Slumbering Cindersloth took off after her.

"You really might want to run now, *Your Majesty,*" they heard Titania call as she fled. "You're supposed to call me 'Your Majesty'!"

And then they were gone.

"What does she mean we could turn into unicorns?" asked Sabledusk, trotting up to them. "Who would want to be a unicorn?"

"Well, actually," explained Midnight, "you are a unicorn. We all are."

"I'm no unicorn," snorted the leader of the Curse.

"Pardon me, ma'am," said Curious. "But you are. You see, the fairy queen was using Pumpkin Jack to collect your horns to make her crown. When Jack found a unicorn alone, one with a really powerful horn, he stole the horn for her. But the horn is what focuses a unicorn's magic. Without a focus, your magic comes out all diffused and fiery. Hard to control. That's what causes your fire. You're all unicorns who have lost their horns."

"That's why we night mares just appear in the Whisperwood," said Midnight.

"But I don't remember being a unicorn," said Sable-dusk.

"What's your earliest memory?" Curious asked Mid-night.

"Running in a sort of dream, blazing fire, and my mother finding me."

"All that unfocused magic blazing out at once burns up your memories," said Curious. "Unicorns are stuck-up. We're prideful. We think a lot of our horns. Losing them is pretty traumatic. So you block it out. You forget what you can never have again."

"But why is Jack after our horns?" asked Midnight. "The crown wasn't for him."

"No," said Curious. "Jack rode each of you on the night he stole your horn. Somehow, when all that magic was re-leased, he used it to enter the dreams of sleeping people. He told us himself that he fed on nightmares. It was that ability to open doorways to other places that he harnessed to send the stones away. He didn't need the crown at all. He only wanted a whole herd of night mares and a bunch of Absorbing Orbs full of wispy wood winks. Helping the queen build the crown was just cover for his own plan."

"So," said Sabledusk, "if we're all unicorns . . . that's going to take some getting used to."

"For us too," said Curious. "But when I tell Goldenmane,

I think he'll want to reexamine the way we've been doing things. I don't know, but I think that maybe this could be a new beginning."

"It's certainly not an ending," said Midnight. "There's still a lot to be done."

But it was an ending, of sorts. And in the end, Midnight left the stones alone. To keep the Curse safe at night, without driving out the entire forest of Wicked Fairies. And Midnight gave each of the members of the herd a choice. Some of the night mares in the Curse wanted to be unicorns again. She healed them, and they were. The new night mare was one of them, and Curious wasn't at all surprised to find that she was his friend Grace.

Vision, however, stayed a night mare. As did Sabledusk. In fact, most of the Curse chose to stay as they were and live in the Whisperwood.

But the wood itself had changed. Now green things grew. There were even some flowers among the thistles. But some new things had appeared too, strange creatures that had slipped through from Elsewhither. The Whisperwood was both more beautiful and more mysterious than it had been. And that was okay too.

Only now it had visitors. You can bet that when the unicorns of the Blessing met the new unicorns of the Curse, they were surprised. Several of them recognized old friends and family that had disappeared long ago. Goldenmane wasn't sure what to make of it, but Poor Mad Tom's raft soon had a lot of work, ferrying unicorns and night mares back and forth across the River Restless. There was even talk of building a bridge. Not a bridge of smoke and memories, like a fairy might build—a proper bridge with wooden planks. Curious thought that it should be a covered one, like the one that had started it all.

As for Queen Titania, she escaped the Slumbering Cindersloth, but she stayed shut up in her palace and didn't show her face. A big black cloud rained over her palace every day, and nowhere else.

As for another fairy, no one reported seeing Jack o' the Hunt anywhere, though they searched for him high and low. Perhaps he was really gone. Perhaps not.

Curious and Midnight saw each other as often as they could. Curious kept the horseshoe. It didn't bother him anymore, and it certainly had its uses. But Midnight didn't think anyone should keep the Crown of Horns. So one day, when she had healed everyone who wanted healing and was certain all the work was done, she asked her friend to meet her.

"Are you sure about this?" Curious asked her as they stood on the banks of the River Restless. "I mean, you were a unicorn before Jack stole your horn."

Midnight laughed. "I am a unicorn still." Then she neighed and tossed her head. "That sounds so strange. I always hated unicorns. Now I'm best friends with one."

"Best friends?" said Curious. And he stamped his feet nervously.

"Of course, you idiot," she said. "Hasn't your Scientific Mind worked that out already?"

Curious smiled.

"Sometimes a Scientific Mind needs a Scientific Heart."

He nudged the Crown of Horns with a hoof. It was sitting on a rock by the shore.

"So, time for the Experiment, then," he said.

"Time for the Plan, you mean."

"If you're sure you're sure."

"Oh, yes."

"How are you going to do this?"

"How do you think? I'm going to Stomp!"

Midnight lifted her hoof high in the air. She brought her hoof down hard, and she smashed the Crown of Horns. She smashed it to bits.

Together, they gathered up the remains in their teeth and tossed them into the river. Then they stood together on the shore. It no longer mattered what side of the water they were on. So I won't bother telling you.

⚜ ACKNOWLEDGMENTS ⚜

Once Upon a Unicorn couldn't have been written without the enthusiastic input of my daughter, who has read every version of the book multiple times and has been very free in her criticism as well as her praise. I owe her for the idea of Tangleheads and some other neat bits and bobs that made their way into the manuscript.

My wonderful early readers also deserve a mention. Huge thanks for the valuable feedback from Janica York Carter, Rebekah Carter, Jessie Carter, Abigail Tassin, and Terry C. Simpson and his daughter, Kai.

I'm also indebted to my friend Mark Chadbourn. Mark is a writer of adult fantasy books, many of which deal with the Good Neighbors of Celtic mythology. His fairies are much scarier than mine, but his work gave me a love for the fey and their myriad magical courts.

I should acknowledge the work of Henry Fuseli as well. Fuseli was a Swiss painter who, in 1781, produced a painting called *The Nightmare*, which was the first time anyone made the connection between *mare* the word for a female horse and the *mare* in *nightmare*. *The Nightmare* shows a sleeping woman being tormented by an evil spirit, while a somewhat sinister and, I think, rather goofy-looking black horse watches from the shadows. It's because of Fuseli's painting that the idea of evil black horses called nightmares entered into folktales and fantasy.

Which brings me to the debt I owe to my father and to musician Johnny Cash. One of my dad's favorite songs has always been "Ghost Riders in the Sky." It's a song about cowboys doomed to chase the Devil's herd forever, riding through the clouds on "horses snorting fire." I'm not a very big country music fan, and neither is my father, but that song has fascinated me since he first played it for me when I was very young. So I suppose night mares have been in me ever since Dad and Johnny put them there, looking for a chance to come out.

Thanks to my editor at Crown Books for Young Readers, Phoebe Yeh, and to Random House Children's Books publisher Barbara Marcus. Thanks to Elizabeth Stranahan, assistant editor; Josh Redlich, senior publicist; Alison Kolani, director of copyediting; April Ward, art director; and Michelle Cunningham, designer.

I've already mentioned my daughter, but finally, and most important, colossal thanks to my entire family. Without them, my life really would be a nightmare and not the wonderful, unicorn-filled experience that it is.

ABOUT THE AUTHOR

LOU ANDERS is the author of the Thrones and Bones series of fantasy adventure novels, *Frostborn*, *Nightborn*, and *Skyborn*, as well as the novel *Star Wars: Pirate's Price*. In 2016, he was named a Thurber House Writer-in-Residence and spent a month in Columbus, Ohio, teaching, writing, and living in a haunted house. A prolific speaker, Anders regularly makes school visits and attends literary festivals and writing conventions around the country. When not writing, he enjoys role-playing games, 3-D printing, and watching movies. He lives with his family and a goldendoodle in Birmingham, Alabama.

LOUANDERS.COM

Play the game. Save the empire.
The adventure starts here.

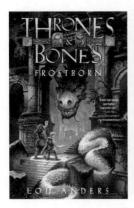

A *School Library Journal* YA and Middle Grade
Reads for *Game of Thrones* Fans Selection!

AVAILABLE NOW!